THE
Preacher's
LADY

Also by Lori Copeland

The Seattle Brides Series
With Virginia Smith

A Bride for Noah
Rainy Day Dreams

The Amish of Apple Grove Series
With Virginia Smith

The Heart's Frontier
A Plain and Simple Heart
A Cowboy at Heart

The Dakota Diaries
Love Blooms in Winter
Under the Summer Sky

Standalone Novels
Sisters of Mercy Flats
My Heart Stood Still
The Healer's Touch
When Love Comes My Way

THE
Preacher's
LADY

LORI
COPELAND

HARVEST HOUSE PUBLISHERS
EUGENE, OREGON

All Scripture quotations are taken from the King James Version of the Bible.

Cover by Left Coast Design, Portland, Oregon

Cover photo © Dragon Images / Shutterstock

Published in association with the Books & Such Management, 52 Mission Circle, Suite 122, PMB 170, Santa Rosa, CA 95409-5370, www.booksandsuch.com.

Library of Congress Cataloging-in-Publication Data
    Copeland, Lori.
    The preacher's lady / Lori Copeland.
    pages ; cm. — (Sugar maple hearts ; Book 1)
    ISBN 978-0-7369-5655-0 (pbk.)
    ISBN 978-0-7369-5656-7 (eBook)
    I. Title.
    PS3553.O6336P74 2016
    813'.54—dc23

                                                2015021166

Printed in the United States of America

        16 17 18 19 20 21 22 23 24 / BP- JH / 10 9 8 7 6 5 4 3 2 1

Prologue

Berrytop, Wisconsin
1877

"Listen up, Wisconsin!" The young man inched farther out on the pine's reaching branches and cupped his hands to his mouth to shout at the top of his lungs. "Bo Garrett is helplessly, don't-care-who-knows-it in love with Elly Sullivan!"

His words echoed over the snowy meadow. Deer scattered toward the far woods, where the heavy snows of Wisconsin lay on burdened limbs.

Grinning, the young woman climbed to join Bo and shouted louder. "Elly Sullivan is madly, wildly, forever, out-of-her-mind in love with Bo Garrett!"

The wind snatched her words and tossed them through a mist of swirling snow. Bo tipped his head toward the ground, and they climbed down together. He took her hand to walk to the leafless maple that stood atop the rise. He dug deep in his pocket for his knife and carefully etched the initials BG + ES in the trunk. Decades of carved vows covered the ancient bole. The permanence of Bo's promise warmed Elly.

The young couple couldn't stay somber for long. They dissolved into laughter over their heady declarations and fell spread-eagle in the snow to stare at the pressing overcast sky. Even with the threat of another storm, Elly held the moment tightly. To hear Bo's words, spoken with such surety, was sheer bliss. When Bo, this soon-to-be man, turned seventeen, they would get married, they would have beautiful babies, and life would be perfect.

Rolling to his side, Bo playfully ruffled the chestnut curls that sprang from Elly's bonnet, his eyes softening with a rare intensity. "I'm fifteen now, but in one year, nine months, thirteen days and"— he pulled a watch fob from his pocket and squinted—"eight minutes, you will be my wife."

She sat up and Bo helped her to stand. She stroked his wind-chapped cheek, where shoots of a reddish-blond beard sprouted. "Lots of kids get married earlier. Rose and Jack were barely sixteen, and they have a baby."

"That's not the way to do it, Elly. I don't know about you, but I'm not ready for babies yet."

"No." She snuggled closer to his warmth. "Neither am I. But the babies could come later."

Shaking his head, he refused the notion. "I know they could, but I'm not settled enough. I'm still in school and I want to finish my learning. Pa says a man needs an education in order to get ahead these days."

"Not to raise cranberries," she argued. The Garrett and Sullivan families owned two of the largest bogs in these parts, and Pa had barely finished sixth grade when he'd gone to work. Raising cranberries had been a Sullivan legacy for generations. Elly couldn't imagine doing anything else.

If she was patient, Bo would see the wisdom of following in the footsteps of their families. And on the day he turned seventeen, he would marry her, and like everybody around Berrytop, come fall they'd harvest cranberries. Fat little balls that bounced as high as a tabletop. They also stung like wildfire when thrown with enough velocity. She'd been Bo's target in many a cranberry fight. The memory brought a smile to her face.

She tightened her arms around him, feeling the warmth of him through her coat. If only time passed faster. Two years felt like centuries when all she wanted in life was to be his wife, the mother of his babies, the keeper of his heart.

Gazes lifted to the sky to watch the dizzying dance of falling snow. Winter trudged on endlessly in these parts. Their last chance to be together would be the church social Saturday night, and after that who knew when they'd be able to do little more than wave at each other from their bedroom windows? "Think the weather will hold for Saturday night?" she asked.

He smiled. "Sure hope so. So far it's been right pleasant for January. This little storm isn't going to be much. If we're lucky—"

"Why do you say *lucky*?" She lightly swatted his arm. "You should say *blessed*. The Lord has *blessed* us with decent weather."

"Blessed us?" He threw back his head and hooted, white teeth flashing. "Since when does Elly Sullivan talk about blessings?"

She gave him another punch accompanied by a dour look. Teasing about such things seemed dangerous.

"You know I don't hold with religious talk," he said. "You sound like the preacher's wife." Reverend Ed and Myrtle Richardson (dubbed "Reverend and Mrs. Righteous" by the younger crowd) were always harping on the proper use of words.

Reverend Ed had roared from the pulpit, "There is no such thing as luck! You receive a blessing from the Almighty!" Sweat rolled down his temples, and his face turned fiery red. Often he shouted so loud that windows slammed shut. Old Mr. Vaughn patiently got up, shuffled to the panes, and lifted them back into place.

One day Vaughn got the idea to cut some strong wooden sticks to prop the panels open. From then on there hadn't been anything to deter the Reverend from his pious fury.

Grinning, Elly breathed in the scent of smoke, coffee, and bacon from Bo's coat, putting church out of her mind. She still had two whole days to steel herself for the coming wrath of Reverend Richardson's sermon. "Promise me one thing, Bo Garrett. Promise me you'll *never* be a preacher," she whispered.

Chuckling, he tightened his arms around her. "Do I act like a preacher to you?"

"No, but you make it through Richardson's sermons without running for your life."

"Are you telling me that big, loud man scares you?" He playfully tweaked her nose.

She wasn't amused. "Yes, he scares me. Scares me half to death, Bo. Makes me wonder...If God is so petulant and so out to get me, I wonder why I should even worship Him."

"Now come on. God isn't petulant or out to get anyone. Just because Richardson likes to hear the sound of his own voice doesn't mean God isn't what He claims to be. If Richardson makes Him sound tough, well, I suppose He is if His children disobey, but since He created us I guess He has the right to do what He wants." Pushing his hat back, he fixed his blue eyes on her. "You're serious, aren't you? You're afraid of God?"

"I'm very serious. Pastor terrifies me. I would rather stay home Sundays and not feel so threatened."

His grin faded. "You believe in God, don't you?"

She shook her head. "I'm not sure anymore, but I'd never let Pa hear me say it."

Shaking his head, he pulled her close. "Elly Sullivan. What is the world coming to? I've never heard you doubt God's existence."

"I'm dead serious." She broke the embrace and brushed at the snow accumulating on her shoulders. It felt good to tell Bo her feelings. All her life she'd gone along with the ritual: church on Sunday and Wednesday night, weather permitting. But lately Richardson's sermons had been grating on her; made her doubt her belief. "Who in their right mind would believe in a mystical being that makes people miserable?"

"That isn't God's intention."

She didn't like defending herself against God, but the words spilled out. "How can you say that? All that pounding and screaming and yelling from Reverend Richardson makes me feel like I've spent two hours in the very hell he claims is my ultimate destination."

"Well, some folk have a way of getting riled up about the message." He pulled her collar up and tightened her scarf. "Me, I believe what he preaches. Take this snow, for instance, and the trees—the way they seem to die in the fall only to come back to life in the spring, radiant with new growth. Take the workings of the human body. Who but God could make anything so intricate?" He opened his arms to frame the expanse of sky. "All of this is far beyond man's ability."

She shook her head. Bo had sat through the same sermons she had, Sunday after Sunday, hearing nothing but doom and gloom, certainly very little about blessings. She met his lake-blue eyes for some hint of teasing. There was none.

Struggling to her feet, she stomped to pulse some warmth into her feet. "Do you really believe there is such a God, that there's a special—I don't know, something or someone—who sits on high and watches over us, someone who would give His own flesh to spare our sinful souls?" She snorted her disbelief.

"I do, Elly. I believe every word of the Bible. I still have questions, but the story does make you stop to think."

"Who can think with all that screaming and hollering going on from the pulpit? It makes me want to run and hide in shame."

He gathered her close and kissed her long and sweet.

"Bo," she whispered against his lips, "you didn't agree not to be a preacher."

Laughing, he kissed her again. "I think that's a pretty safe wager."

"Better not let Richardson hear you say *wager*."

"Right, I'll only mention blessings when he's around." Their lips met and lingered. Soft, loving touches on the neck, at the base of the ears. Snow began to fall in earnest now. He gazed at her. "I love you so much it hurts."

Nodding, she whispered, "Two years is a long time. Will you promise me one more thing?" she asked.

"Anything you want."

"Promise to never love another?" She knew asking him for such a pledge was unfair and most highly speculative, even with all their talk of forever love and marriage. What she felt now would never change, but Bo could change.

His gaze fastened to hers. "I will never love anyone but you, Elly Sullivan. I promise."

"Do you want the same promise from me?"

"Nah." A smug smile spread across his wind-chapped features. "You'll wait for me. Who in their right mind would let me go?"

She playfully swatted his shoulder again. "You conceited boor. How do you know someone won't come along and sweep me off my feet? Gideon Long, Hank Martin, Rex Pierson...? Who knows? I might forget all about you, Mr. Garrett."

Catching her hands, he clutched them tightly to his chest, where she could feel the steady thrum of his heartbeat. He spoke from a deep place. "This heart beats for you and you alone. You asked if

I believe in God? I believe this much: You and I are meant to be together, here, on this earth. You will be the mother of my children. As long as this heart beats in my chest, it will belong only to you."

Lifting her face to his, they sealed the promise with an extended kiss.

Nothing in this world would, or ever could, separate them.

Chapter 1

Berrytop, Wisconsin
1884

Elly ran a finger down her shopping list. With her mother nursing Auntie back to health in Minnesota, household duties at the Sullivans' cranberry farm fell to her. She'd already burned more food than she'd prepared for the table, so she had to keep the menus simple but edible. Pa warned her to stick to the basics.

Adele Garrett, her best friend, leaned in, her eyes bright with conspiracy. Such glee had been a stranger to Adele's face. First morning sickness had gripped her, and then the sorrow of her husband, Ike's, untimely passing. Seeing Adele more like herself lowered Elly's guard this morning.

"Guess what?" Adele whispered.

Elly had waited years—what seemed like a lifetime—to see the truth of what she'd dreamed in Adele's face. "Bo's back," Elly said as she tried to reconcile why his return would be more painful than his leaving. She closed her eyes and drew a deep breath. Somehow she would get through this.

Adele crooked a reddish-blonde brow and frowned, obviously disappointed. "You've seen him?"

"No, and I hope I don't have to." Uttering those words to Bo's sister was the most hurtful thing she could have spoken. Adele, with her awful loss and troubles, didn't deserve Elly's bite. But Bo sure did.

Elly reached for her friend's hand. "I'm sorry. I can be so hateful. But you know Bo stopped writing years ago. I heard nothing for all these years—seven years, Adele. How would you feel? For all I knew, he could have been dead." She stopped, swallowed, and dropped Adele's hand. "For all I know he's married and has children." She stepped around Adele and reached for a box of salt. The mere thought of Bo with another woman set her teeth on edge. Would it have *killed* him to write more often?

For years, maybe all of her life, that boy—correction—that *man* had dominated her life. Bo was full-grown now, not the silly love-struck kid who had turned on her like a snake and become a...Her mind chaffed at forming the word.

Preacher.

Bible thumper.

Harp polisher.

Adele shrugged and looked crestfallen. "Sorry. I thought I should warn you."

Elly could not let Adele's tender condition sway her from getting the shopping done and back home, where she could work out her anger on a kneading board. "Consider me properly warned." She slapped the box of salt into her basket. Forewarned was forearmed.

"You don't want to know why he's back?" Adele pressed.

Elly slung a bag of flour into the basket. "Not really." This morning she entertained more worthy thoughts than Bo Garrett. The berries were starting to pink up. That meant harvest wasn't far off. From now until the end of November, she would have nary a thing on her mind but plain old hard work. Most folks around Wisconsin parts tapped maple syrup, but not the Sullivans or their neighbors across the road, the Garretts. The Sullivans grew cranberries. Acres of dry, sandy bogs surrounded their operations, and right now the marshes were mushrooming with berries.

Adele tugged Elly's sleeve. "You honestly don't want to see him?"

"I seriously do not, Adele. I don't care if I never see him again. Will you hand me that tin of coffee?"

A familiar baritone from the front of the mercantile startled her. "Miss Sullivan? If you could speak up a bit? I don't believe the folks outside caught your disdain for me."

Someday, when I'm old enough, I'm going to marry you, Elly Sullivan.

Heat flooded Elly's cheeks. She swung toward the door to see the speaker. His eyes had taken on the brilliant hue of a summer sky. Right now they twinkled at her mischievously. He still stood a good head taller than she—enough that she had once balanced on tiptoes to meet his lips. Thick, sandy-colored hair touched his collar, and he looked the part of a rogue from the stubble of his light beard. Rogue though he be, he still wore denims and a blue-and-white checked shirt. The years had been overly kind to Bo Garrett.

He was still the best-looking man in Berrytop. The world, actually.

She stiffened with resentment and checked her reaction. She could not allow something as inconsequential as a comely face make her forget how he had shattered her heart. Taken it and slammed it against a rock and then took the heel of his boot and ground it into the dirt like a roach.

Fine, that was overdramatic, but he had.

Plus shamelessly lied to her.

His voice softened to one she had heard in her dreams on endless nights. "Hello, Elly." Their eyes met and her knees turned to tree sap.

Flustered, she whirled back to concentrate on the shelves that now swam before her eyes. He'd *heard* her crude remark. And his cocky grin told her he'd not only heard, but that the insult rolled off like water from a duck's back.

When her gaze focused on the coffee, a sun-bronzed arm reached around her, chose a brand, and dropped the tin into her basket. "Easier on the stomach," he said. He moved on, straightened a tin of baking powder, and walked toward the harness section in the back of the store. Thank goodness he had not chosen a public encounter to scold her for her careless words.

And now she couldn't find her voice. His presence had rendered her speechless, which wasn't easy to do.

When she approached the clerk with her items, she realized Adele had quietly excused herself and left, the coward. Elly was alone to face the man she'd sworn never to speak to again.

But she needn't have worried. Bo lingered in the back of the store, so she hurriedly paid for her purchases and trotted out of the store. Releasing a sigh, she crossed the street and walked the short distance home, glancing over her shoulder to be sure she wasn't followed.

Bo was back. She'd stoked a healthy hatred of the man only to turn to mush at the sight of him. Hating someone wasn't quite as easy as she'd imagined.

A groan escaped when she spotted a young woman trying to wave her down. Rosie Meadows. Not only was her name difficult to say without grinning, the young woman was quickly becoming a pest. Seven years ago she was a darling little girl who liked to tag along, but today she was a fourteen-year-old who was quite certain that Elly lived a fairy-tale existence. Though Bo had been gone all these years, Rosie still expected him to ride back someday and swoop Elly up into his arms. And then the two star-crossed lovers would live happily ever after. Elly had tried to explain a hundred times that she and Bo were no more, but Rosie wouldn't believe it. Her head was filled with girlish expectations, and like it or not, Elly and Bo's love was the town legend.

Surely, Rosie stated with a sigh of finality, a love like theirs would *never* "wither away on the vine."

Reversing her steps, Ella headed the opposite direction, but she wasn't surprised when the maneuver failed to deter young Rosie. The young girl hurried to catch up. "Have you seen him yet?"

"Seen whom?"

"*Him*. Bo! He's back."

"Really?" Elly picked up her pace.

"Are you serious? Bo's *back*." Rosie reached to halt Elly's steps. "What's wrong with you?"

"Wrong? There's nothing wrong. I need to get home and fix Pa's dinner." Elly gently released the girl's grasp. "Isn't it your dinner time?"

"Who can think about food at a time like this? Love is in the air!"

More like rotten apples. Elly kept her pace.

"Elly Sullivan, I don't know what to think of you. How can you be so calm and collected when the boy you've loved forever has finally come home?" She fell into step and trailed Elly across the street. "Well, I suppose I can understand your reaction. He's returned so suddenly—you'll surely have a chance to catch up at the church social. It's the last of the season, you know. Everyone will be there—simply everyone. Quint has already asked if I'd take a long walk with him—you know, it's so fascinating that you and Bo fell in love at such an early age, and Quint and I—well, I'm fourteen and he's fifteen but the minute we're old enough we're getting married—"

Elly listened as the young woman prattled on, sowing impossible dreams like handfuls of wildflowers. At the tender age of fourteen, everything seemed possible.

Stepping on the back stoop, Elly turned and smiled. "So nice to see you, Rosie. Give my regards to your folks."

Rosie paused, her cheeks red with exertion. "You *really* haven't seen Bo?"

"I really haven't."

The girl's eyes narrowed. "Have you broken up? You and Bo? The two people in this whole wide world who truly love each other?"

"Yes, we have."

She gave a heated stomp. "When?"

"Actually, Rosie, Bo didn't tell me when. Now hurry along. Your mother needs you in the kitchen."

Elly pushed the door open with her back and left Rosie with a mystified expression. How did you tell a young girl with a head full of dreams to not count on any single one coming true?

Her arms ached under the weight of her purchases as Elly entered the kitchen. The old dwelling had housed Sullivans for generations. The one-story rock house meandered, creating crooks and crannies, enlarging its footprint as each generation added on rooms and service porches.

Various pieces of farm equipment sat poised in the yard, waiting to be utilized when the harvest reached full swing. Bogs stretched across ten acres of Sullivan land. The Garretts presently owned the biggest cranberry operation, twenty prime acres. The Sullivans were their closest rivals.

When the screen door slammed behind Elly, her pa, Holt Sullivan, glanced up from reading the newspaper. He'd been scribbling figures in his journal, most likely the prices for bushels of cranberries.

"Elly? Are your pants on fire, girl?"

"No." She stalked across the kitchen floor, carrying the bulky parcels of goods, and headed for the pantry. *Young, foolish girls falling in love, thinking their emotions would last forever, thinking promises made during moonlit walks would actually be fulfilled.* Nothing but silly speculations fed by spirited boys who had no intention of keeping their promises.

"Elly?"

She was in no mood for Pa's teasing. How many times had she reminded him to adjust the spring on the screen door? Honestly, nothing got done around here with Ma gone. Pa would never let a heartbeat skip before doing what Ma asked of him. But now, seasons would change before he got around to mundane chores.

Despite his reticence for mending doors and such, Elly adored the man. He still sported a headful of wavy hair, clearly the contributor of Elly's richly colored locks. Even in his middle years, his back stood erect to support broad shoulders. He'd worked hard to build the farm, and he wore the evidence of his toil in his muscled form.

Pa's gaze dropped to the newspaper. "What's for dinner?"

The prices must be good, if he was thinking ahead to dinner and not remembering the chops she'd burned the day before. "Ham and gravy."

He glanced up, disappointment weighing his features. "But it's Wednesday."

Since she could remember, Ma had made beans and cornbread for dinner Wednesdays. She'd thought Papa would appreciate a change. Evidently, he liked the rigid menu. "Beans and cornbread, then," she said with resignation.

His voice lightened. "Got a letter from Ma today."

Elly glanced up as she poured the flour into a chipped crock. It had been weeks since Ma had left to tend her aunt when a summer cold had turned into pneumonia. Elly rested her hands on the bundle. "How is Aunt Milly? Will Ma be home soon?"

"Aunt Milly is coming along. Your ma has a way with healing. She says Milly will be up and around in no time." A touch of relief colored his tone.

"That's good." Elly missed Ma and she was sure Pa missed her even more. Since Uncle George passed, Aunt Milly had needed Ma's help often. Her mother had answered the call to go to Minnesota yet again, assuring Elly and her father she would be back before they missed her.

Well, that hadn't happened and harvest was upon them. She had missed Ma since the first day, and no end was in sight. With her around, the old house smelled of warm bread and fresh pies. These days it smelled of neglect and burnt toast, even though Elly was trying her hardest to stay ahead of the workload.

What she missed most of all was Ma's hand smoothing her hair when the two hugged goodnight. Irene stood nearly six feet tall and managed to make a home, bake pies, cakes, and bread, plus working long hours in the bogs right alongside Pa. This was the dream of a happy marriage and motherhood Elly held in her heart.

Theirs was the marriage she should have had with Bo Garrett.

Stoking the dying embers, she slid the iron plate into place and moved the bean pot to the front of the cookstove.

Her father glanced up from his ciphering. "I hear Bo's back. Hope to see the boy in church Sunday."

Bo. Even in her own house she couldn't find peace from that name. After all these years, his name stung like a wasp, but even she couldn't say why. Yes, he'd broken her heart by not coming back. And she loathed the thought of him striking off to see a small part of the world before he settled down. He wouldn't be gone long, he'd said. Just a while.

Seven years?

She didn't know his meaning of *a while*, but hers was entirely different.

It wasn't as though she hadn't tried to forget him and his worthless promises. She'd courted almost every single man in the county, even a couple of widowers, but no one filled the empty hole in her heart. And now he was back. How would she ever face him? Surely he didn't think that she had waited all these long years for him. He was smarter than that.

If she were wise, she would accept Gideon Long's marriage proposal and start a family. She wasn't getting any younger. A couple of children underfoot would erase Bo's memory, but she couldn't marry for children alone. She wanted the kind of wildly exciting love that she and Bo once shared. In truth, she couldn't fathom any man other than Bo to father her babies. And there roosted a perplexing problem.

Elly Sullivan! Where is your respect? Your grit? He's back. You saw him with your own eyes. March over to the Garrett place and ask where he's been all these years. What happened to the declaration that he loved you forever? That he would be back shortly? There was a time you could talk about anything. Nothing was off-limits, and surely not your feelings for each other.

She stiffened her back. She wouldn't ask that man for so much as the time of day, especially when he'd turned into such a low-down deceiver.

She stoked the flame under the bean pot, trying with all of her might to focus on dinner and not Bo Garrett. One hope remained. He would attend to whatever had brought him back to Berrytop and return to wherever he'd been all this time, and do so quickly.

Pa tilted his chair back. "I been hearing the Reverend's gonna preach on hell this week. That's good. Folks need to hear more sermons on the subject."

Elly rolled her eyes. Papa was a good man. Why did he take such delight—practically wringing his hands in pleasure—in hearing that some people were bound to burn in an eternal fire? Yet she couldn't get too upset with him. Pa only echoed what he heard every Sunday in church. Unfortunately, she heard it all too, and took no such delight in anyone's impending doom.

Not a single unsaved soul sat in Pastor Richardson's pews on Sunday mornings. Just once she would like to hear encouraging words, like the stories Ma used to tell at bedtime of a God who suffered in His children's stead. She spoke of a God born into this world to love, not to scare folks. Ma always said you could win more souls with honey than persimmons. The Reverend had Elly so confused about what she did believe and what she didn't believe that she dreaded Sundays.

"Yes, sir." Her father's chair hit the floor with a thud. "Someone needs to set a fire under these folks. They're too lax."

"How so, Pa?" She knew the answer, but she never missed the chance to challenge him.

"Because they go their ways ignoring God, never give Him a moment's thought except when they get in a fix and need Him. *Then* He hears from them all right! Oh Lordy, Lordy, help me! I need your grace now!"

"Which He unfailingly gives," she murmured under her breath. "Now, Pa, what is that Scripture exactly? 'Judge not, and ye shall not be judged'—something like that?"

"What I'm sayin' is different, smarty pants. The truth is as plain as the nose on your face. Some folks turn their backs on the good Lord until they need Him, and then if He doesn't answer right away they say that proves He isn't there."

He stood and folded his newspaper. "It so happens your pa sees things with his own eyes. Folks don't make the slightest effort to attend services when the weather gets bad. They stay home and roast their toes before the fire like heathens."

"Even old Mrs. Snell?" Elly asked, expecting she'd caught him this time. No one in the county lived more saintly than Mrs. Snell. She'd been attending the sick and taking in orphans and visiting newcomers with baskets of home-baked goodness since long before the Reverend came to town. She even brought Pa's favorite, cinnamon rolls, when he twisted his ankle two seasons ago. Many a time Edith Snell had shown up on a cold, snowy day to bring the Sullivans something fresh out of the oven.

"Mrs. Snell can surely make it into town if she runs low on sugar. No siree, church attendance drops off if the weather isn't fittin'. But we're there. Preacher can always count on us."

Yes, her family was always in their pew. Through sickness, deplorable weather, and bone-biting weariness, the Sullivans were faithfully in church to hear the wrath of God meted out Sunday after Sunday. It seemed to Elly that no matter how hard she tried to live right, confess her sin, and accept God as her Savior, she balanced on the brink of damnation. Years ago, she had stopped trying to make sense of the fury. She now attended church services because Pa required her to do so, not because she expected any sort of encouragement or revelation. When the preacher yelled, turned red in the face, and spoke of a vengeful deity, she wrapped her hands around her stomach and mentally removed herself from the pew.

The God who tempted her belief wasn't mean or angry. He was faithful, meant what He said, would dole out punishment when necessary, and didn't much care for folks who tried to step in and replace Him. Hers was the God Ma had told her about, who had died for her sins, and only by His grace would she ever step one foot in heaven. Not by her works. Not by her attendance in a building. Not by judging dear friends who took a Sunday off. Certainly only through shed blood would she enter the gates of heaven. Hers was a completely different God from the one the Reverend spat about.

"What this town needs is a good revival." Pa pounded the table with his fist. "That would set a few of these folks straight and jerk a knot in their tails."

Elly longed to change the direction of this conversation. "Do you want coffee or tea with dinner?"

"Coffee's fine. There's still some in the pot." He walked to the door and settled his hat on his head. "I'm headin' over to invite Bo to Sunday services. No doubt he could use a good talking-to for all the heartache he's caused Milt and Faye." He paused and turned to look at her. "Have you seen him?"

"Briefly."

"I guess..." He shook his head. "Guess you and him are history."

"Correct."

"Well, he needs to be in church. Think I'll go over and talk politics with Milt."

Closing her eyes, Ella whispered, "Don't let Milt be home." Every election year was a nightmare. If her father favored a candidate you could bet Milt wouldn't. And this year's candidates had started a small war between the men. Thank goodness November was in sight, and nobody would have to listen to the political bluster much longer.

Elly fished a piece of salt pork out of the beans with a ladle and remembered something else. Obviously, Pa hadn't heard of Bo's new calling.

Chapter 2

Bo followed Jeremiah to the kitchen door of his parents' home, where the child parted ways and ran toward the barn to find the kittens born during the night. The foreman's son was a bit hard to keep up with.

Bo pulled off his muddy boots before stepping into his mother's kitchen. He found her hefting a pot of coffee from the stove.

"Ma? What's going on? I'm right in the middle of loading."

"Time for coffee, of course."

She carried the coffeepot to the table. Bo didn't try to argue with her. He gathered the mugs and the cream and sugar Ma liked, not that he ever turned away anything sweet.

Faye filled the mugs and returned the pot to the stove. "You've had a chance to watch your father work. How's he holding up?"

Bo shrugged. "He's resting more, not so anyone would notice if they weren't paying attention. I caught him leaning on his shovel. He seems to be stopping more often." Bo considered her reaction if he told her everything, that he wasn't the old Pa, that he sat more often, took more breaks, but he held up. She was worried enough about Pa's health. "I'd say he's the same ol' Pa; just getting a little older."

"Have mercy. That man is going to be the death of me. Bo, we have to get him to slow down. His heart won't take the strain. The doctor warned him about pushing too hard."

The two sat down at the scarred table. "He'll be fine," said Bo. "You know how stubborn he is. I don't know why he feels the need for all this secrecy. If his heart's failing, there's no crime committed. And pride will send him to an early grave."

"Pride." Faye wrapped her hands around the mug of coffee to warm them. "Yes, there's a great deal of pride in him. I know he fights the notion, but there is. He would have my hide if he thought we were talking behind his back." Water gathered in the corners of her eye. "I can't bear the thought of losing him."

Losing one or both parents was inconceivable, but how many times in the past year had Bo stood at a graveside and comforted a grieving family? Far too many, and now it seemed the Grim Reaper had followed him home.

Faye squeezed his hand. "Thank you for coming. You're just what your father needs—good for his soul and good for his heart."

Guilt washed over Bo. "Ma. I meant to write more—"

"But you never got around to it." Her soft chuckle stirred boyhood memories. No one knew him better. And no one had more to forgive than Ma—with the exception of Elly. Ma never said so, but his years of absence and silence could not have been easy on her. He deeply regretted his reckless youth, and now Pa was sick.

How different his life would be if he had stayed here, married the love of his life, and done his share of the work. He couldn't have prevented Pa's failing heart, but he sure could have stopped Elly's hurt all these years. The way she had looked at him in the mercantile...the raw betrayal in her eyes...

His gaze roamed the room. The old cookstove, warped cabinets, worn floor. Ma kept a clean house, but some things couldn't be made presentable. This old kitchen and disfigured table had been the centerpiece of many a conversation and a few heated lectures. When he'd ridden off that day, he'd planned to come back soon, marry Elly, and build a new home big enough to hold Ma and Pa when they got old and unable to work. What had happened to Bo Garrett's dreams? What had happened to the young idealist who rode away and returned a broken man, who but for God's grace would have been six feet under?

The ache in his heart momentarily lessened and a grin formed on his lips. "I suppose you were a little surprised to learn that I'm preaching now."

"Not in the least." She reached for the cream pitcher. "I know my boy. You had a lot of figuring out to do before you accepted the Lord's call, but I knew it would come someday." She spooned two teaspoons of sugar into her cup. "Being a preacher makes you one of His most ardent supporters. I like that."

If she only knew how long it had taken him to turn back to God. "Well, I guess getting older straightens a man's thoughts and heart. Time to stop carousing and think about the future. I don't know where I thought I was headed before He intervened in my life."

Ma peered at him over her glasses. "I suppose you got yourself into plenty of nonsense you don't care to tell me about."

She'd already figured out more than he wanted her to know. Ma knew man's nature, but she was discreet enough to leave the subject for another time. Left to his own devices, he most likely wouldn't be sitting in her kitchen, drinking her coffee.

"Anything you should tell me? Anything likely to come back to haunt the family?"

It was the question he'd most dreaded, the one that kept him staring at the ceiling many nights. "Ma, I love you, but I don't know the answer to that question. I suppose anything's possible. I'm praying real hard you'll never have to know a minute of my other life."

"What about Elly?"

"Elly." He took a long sip of his coffee.

"Is it over?"

He lifted a dubious brow. "What do you think?"

"I think you made the biggest mistake of your life, but it's over. Life goes on." Faye sobered. "We have some serious talking to do. We won't often have time to ourselves to consider the future in the next few weeks."

He braced himself. There was a reason he'd been traced down and handed a letter a month ago. He'd speculated the reason for his summons home, knowing that whatever it was, the matter was serious. Only Ma had known his whereabouts the past couple of years, and he'd sworn her to secrecy. He was working hard to overcome his wrongs, but echoes of his past still plagued him. In time he'd planned to come back—to face Elly...

Ma continued. "To be truthful, your pa could keel over at any moment. I know that's harsh, but that's the reality we have to deal with. I have Rodney. He's a fine foreman, but he isn't a son with a vested interest in the success of the farm, and he isn't always as attentive to details as he needs to be. I haven't told Anne how bad Pa is looking—didn't see that she could do anything about it. And we're supporting Adele, and soon there will be a baby needing clothes and the like." Ma bit her lower lip in concentration. "We need you here, Bo. I need you here." Her hand tightened in his. "Can I count on you?"

The inevitable tug-of-war started. He hadn't planned on staying. New believers filled his church in Parsons, Kansas. Those turned away by other churches had found a home in the clapboard building he pastored. What would become of these misfits who, after only two years of teaching, were beginning to understand the power of grace? They deserved his loyalty.

Ma scooted her chair back to retrieve the coffeepot. "Adele's had so much grief in her short life. I think she suspects Pa is ailing, but we haven't discussed the matter. She's so very close to your father. And Anne lives so far away she couldn't do a thing to help. Better that both girls have this precious time to enjoy their innocence."

Bo wasn't sure how he would work it out, but he would. "Of course I'll be here. For as long as you need me."

Once again, he was a cranberry farmer. His heart would be in Parsons, but his family needed him. He could get his deacon to fill in for the short harvest season.

Ma interrupted his thoughts. "The only thing your father needs is peace of mind. You know what a worrier he is, and if you're wondering about his eternal state—"

"No, I know he's in good standing with the Lord." Pa wasn't necessarily in church every time the doors opened, but he made no secret of his belief in the Almighty. His life was a testament to compassion, love, and patience—though the latter was his nature, not what he banked his soul on.

Bo remembered his father's booming voice taking a man to task when he bragged about his good works. "Good works might get you a pat on the back, but when it comes to your salvation, you might as well skip rocks in the stream. Nothing is gonna get you to heaven but the shed blood of God."

How many times had Bo used the very same words in his sermons? Lately, he'd noticed he was sounding more and more like Milt.

"He's always depended on me to handle the finances. I can run that end of the business as well or better than any man. What I need is someone out there, in the bogs, keeping an eye on things. Knowing you're home will ease his mind mightily." Ma's gaze pierced him. "Is there anything more important than letting your father go in peace?"

Bo had never dreamed she'd ask that he stay. Staying meant walking away from the new life he'd built, and he couldn't do that either. If Pa improved, he could ride away with a lighter conscience.

Elly came to mind like she always did, but he didn't have a grain of hope with her anymore. The moment he told her where and what he'd been doing all these years, she would walk away without a backward glance. Only she'd smack him a good one first.

"I'll help in any way I can."

"My boy, a preacher." Faye reached up to stroke his hair. "You need a haircut."

Now she sounded like Ma. He pushed his chair back. "I've been busy. There's a lot of sickness in the flock, even a couple deaths."

Ma joined him at the door. "You're too thin. A few suppers of pork chops and fried chicken and you'll fatten up."

Shaking his head, he wondered if a mother ever stopped clucking over her baby chicks. He flashed a grin. "I'd better get back before Pa threatens to tan my hide." He took Ma's work-worn hand in his. "I'll send a wire to let the church know I'll be away for a while. You can count on me."

His gaze drifted toward the Sullivan farm. The words of his youth nagged him: *Bo Garrett is hopelessly, helplessly in love with Elly Sullivan and don't care who knows it!*

And still was, for that matter.

He'd changed since he and Elly stood on that hill and declared eternal love, though his love for her hadn't changed an iota. His heart was still hers. He knew it the moment he saw her in the mercantile. He'd known it all along. But judging by her embittered stare, she no longer returned the sentiment.

Did she know he was a preacher? Probably. He'd seen that look before and it wasn't her friendliest.

"Promise me one thing."

"Anything."

"You'll never be a preacher."

He'd made the promise in good faith. That day on that hilltop with her, preaching couldn't have been further from his mind. But five years of living for the devil had changed him. Whiskey became more important than religion, wild women more sacred than God's Word, and worldly pleasure more inviting than eternal life. He left his home and Elly to seek adventure, and he found it in all the wrong places. When he fell in with a bunch of cowherders, he discovered a different life—a new town every couple of weeks, gambling, loose women offering favors for money, and a way of talking that would have put Ma in an early grave. He surrendered everything to Satan. Handed his life over on a golden plate.

And yet God pursued him. A fierce storm sprung up as he rode the trail. The cattle stampeded and the race to gather the scattered heifers commenced. Bo had been riding straight into a herd of longhorns when a bolt of lightning hit him and knocked him out of the saddle.

If the lightning bolt had done its job, he would have been a dead man with no hope.

Two days later, he came to and gave serious thought to the hereafter. The truth of his near-demise haunted him. He couldn't deny he'd drifted far from his faith—that God was no longer supreme in his life.

The emptiness of his soul ate at him until he couldn't take it anymore. In the middle of a drive, he reined in his horse, rode to the trail boss, and gave notice. Once the herd reached Wichita and the cattle stood secured in pens, he rode away with two weeks' pay and not a backward glance.

He found a home in the town of Parsons, rented a room, and walked into the first church he'd come across that Sunday morning. Whispering Pines wasn't like any church he'd ever attended. The thirty folks filling the pews came from the roughest parts of society, but he fit right in. He wasn't exactly pristine himself. It wasn't long before the pastor was his best friend, and not long after that he was asked to speak in a nearby church.

He recalled his Bible teaching from childhood, and he still pretty well knew the Word inside and out—at least enough to speak on his belief. That Sunday he had stood nervously before the congregation and cleared his throat. But all his nervousness about saying the wrong thing or leading the people astray dissolved as he started speaking, and the congregation invited Bo to stay on.

By then he wasn't going to argue with God. The Almighty had gotten his attention.

"Is Elly married, Ma?"

"She came close about a year ago, but she backed out a few weeks before the wedding."

Bo had no right to ask, but curiosity won out. "Who'd she intend to marry?"

Ma hesitated before answering. "Gideon Long."

Bo pictured a skinny, knobby-kneed, freckle-faced boy who didn't look strong enough to pull taffy, let alone a plow. Evidently, he'd changed.

Elly had every right to marry another man. She'd understood his restlessness—or said she did. She didn't mind his leaving as long as he returned home before too much time passed. But he hadn't.

Instead, he'd repaid her devotion and love with seven long years of betrayal. He had no call to ever question her decisions.

He had been the fool, not her.

All that was left was to beg her forgiveness and offer a hand in friendship.

He couldn't expect more from her.

Chapter 3

Filtered sunrays spread across the eastern sky as Elly approached the bog with her rake and hoe. The newer three-year-old seedlings looked to be thriving. Soon the plants would put out runners to fill the bed before taking root and sprouting uprights.

In late June, pink and red blossoms had carpeted the marshes. The plants now grew thick in the dry peat soil, sprouting crops heavy with ripening berries.

The Sullivans' three bogs—two large and one smaller—lined the road. A clear stream provided ample water for the crops, even in the heat of summer. The stream crossed the road under a timber bridge where the Garretts drew their water. Though sharing such a vital resource, the two families never squabbled.

Even when Bo left and Elly had cried for weeks, Pa told her often a body was asked to release something they loved. If that thing or person loved them back, they would return. Elly cried harder. Bo wasn't a thing or just any person. He was her life. And he hadn't come back.

Months and years of watching the road for a lone rider proved worthless. Riders came and went, but Bo was never among them.

Mail came and went, but only four letters arrived the first year—short letters without much news at all. And then even those stopped. She hadn't heard a word in six years.

It was rumored that Faye Garrett knew his whereabouts but was keeping the secret close. The knowledge that Faye knew and she didn't only strengthened Elly's resentment. Why couldn't she know his whereabouts? Was he ill? Incapacitated? Years of silence passed and Bo's whereabouts no longer mattered, or so she told herself.

Stepping with care into the sunken terrain, she drew the hoe over her head and gave a mighty swing, uprooting a clump of weeds that thrived in the bogs.

Elly straightened, resting her hand in the small of her back. She recalled days long past when she'd roamed this land looking for arrowheads with Bo. They'd filled baskets with the spear-points and tools of the tribes that had lived in the area. Doing so had made the long, hot days of summer seem like one big treasure hunt.

Bo was home.

She set her jaw and deliberately made her mind blank. She wouldn't think about him. She had put foolish dreams aside long ago. She'd overheard folks at the mercantile saying his visit home would be brief. If she tried, maybe she could avoid him. She wouldn't give him the slightest chance to explain his absence all these years, as if explaining away all that silence was possible.

As far as she was concerned, there was no excuse he could offer. None that she would accept.

Her gaze dropped to the bed of thick vines and winced at the immensity of the task before her in the following weeks. Already a chilly wind blew, and her coat seemed too thin for the brisk air. But harvest time was here, and just yesterday she'd read in Pa's newspaper that a hundred-pound barrel of berries was going for fifty-eight cents in the East this year. Women swore the cranberry was as versatile as rhubarb when added to almost any dish, sweet or savory. The berries added a bright, tart note.

As far as Elly was concerned, nothing topped the tantalizing scent of Ma's spiced cranberry muffins baking in the oven. She sweetened the muffins just right, so the sweet didn't overwhelm the tart. Elly liked the sour bite of the berries. She barely puckered when she ate them straight from the vine.

Her gaze drifted to the house across the road, and her heart double-timed when Bo's tall figure stepped onto the porch, holding a coffee mug. He drank his black, unless he'd changed, but he added four teaspoons of sugar. That much she remembered. She dropped her gaze and whacked another stubborn weed.

She looked up when she heard approaching footsteps. Adele, her rounding stomach more prominent these days, appeared. Leaning on the hoe, Elly watched her best friend and confidante pick her way carefully down the incline that led to the bog.

"You're out early this morning," Elly called.

Nodding, Adele stepped into the bog. Her usually tidy strawberry hair lay in a tangled braid on her shoulder. "I couldn't sleep." She yawned. "I don't know how you do this every morning."

"You've picked berries all your life."

"I know, but I don't know how." Straightening, Adele pressed a hand into the small of her back. "It's getting more uncomfortable."

Flashing a grin, Elly sank the hoe back into the dirt. "Complaining already? And you're only—what?—five and a half months along?"

"Six months. Maybe." Adele corrected. "And I'm not complaining. I love being with child. It's just a whole lot different than I thought it would be."

Elly tugged at a stubborn weed. "Like how?"

"The baby fidgets around like a cat in a pillowcase."

"Naturally. The baby's growing, and space must be starting to get cramped in there."

"And my feet look like sausages. I can't get my shoes on."

Elly bit back a grin when she noted Adele's bare feet. Even in the chill, she refused to wear shoes lately. Friends since early childhood, the two women had been inseparable—even more so since Adele's husband died a year after their marriage. They'd discovered the week before his accident that Adele was expecting.

Adele had never been a chronic complainer, but neither was she long-suffering. There was plenty of agony to go around, but Elly counted sharing Adele's discomfort a privilege.

"I know, you're laughing at me." Adele gave a heavy sigh. "Wait until you're expecting. You'll see it's not a picnic."

Adele didn't know everything Elly held in her heart. She had no way of knowing Elly wasn't in a hurry to tie the knot or do the tiresome courting that led up to a proposal and eventually babies. Even if she were to cave to Gideon's persuasions and marry the handsome cattle farmer, she could hardly imagine having children anytime soon.

Adele's hand dropped from the crook of her back and her eyes scanned the bogs. "Having Bo home has made Ma happier, and Pa seems relieved, but they're not telling me something. I'm going to corner Bo and get the truth of all these whispered conversations and sly looks. If he'll slow down enough, I can get him to talk. Now that I'm a widow and a mother-to-be, he won't be able to resist me. He could never deny a helpless female." She paused, her gaze sweeping the Garrett house across the road.

"If you're looking for him now, you just missed him. I glimpsed him coming out of the house earlier." Elly kept her head bent to her work. She didn't want Adele to see any trace of emotion—loathing, lingering infatuation, whichever.

Shading her eyes, Adele scanned her house. "There he is—coming out of the shed." She waved to catch Bo's attention. Elly inwardly groaned. Bo either was avoiding his sister or he didn't see the motion because he walked toward his family's bogs.

"If he thinks I can be avoided that easily, he has another think coming." Adele furrowed her brow. "Something besides the baby tumbling about kept me awake last night." She reached out to still Elly's hoe. "Listen to me. Bo is my brother and I adore him, but what he did to you——to all of us—was selfish and just plain unkind. So you can't let Bo's coming back throw you off the path. Gideon adores you, and he would be the last person to walk out on you. He has more than proven his faithfulness."

Elly met her friend's earnest eyes. "You aren't telling me anything I haven't already considered. Bo is the past, I promise. We were young. Our promises were only childish whims. I see that now." At the time she'd believed every word, hung on Bo's every utterance. "Adele, please don't press me to accept Gideon's proposal. I will when I'm ready. I promise."

"You promised to marry Gideon once before and backed out. What am I supposed to believe? I'm only concerned for your happiness. You're my dearest friend."

Elly didn't appreciate being reminded of her fickle actions. Gideon was all Adele said and more, but she needed more time to make Gideon the man of her dreams. "And I love you to death, Adele. You understand I wasn't ready to marry. Better to back out than make a mistake."

"You broke poor Gideon's heart." Adele's voice held an accusing tone. Strained silence followed, but Elly held her tongue. Since Ike passed, Elly had indulged her friend's meddling ways. If tinkering with Elly's life eased Adele's heartache, so be it.

Adele yawned. "I better catch Bo before he gets too involved in work. I want some answers. Something isn't right around the house and nobody will tell me anything." She kissed Elly on the cheek. "Then I'm going to take a long nap and be nice and fresh for the church supper tonight. You might do the same. It's the last one for a while."

This was new. Adele hadn't done much socializing beyond what was expected since Ike died, and Elly was glad to see her getting out again. The church always met for a picnic before the harvest. The following weeks and months would be filled with work and very little socializing.

Elly never particularly enjoyed the fall function, and for a moment she entertained the notion of not attending anymore church suppers. Starting tonight, she just wouldn't go. She'd go home, heat kettles of hot water for a bath, and soak in the old washtub for a good hour before she dropped into bed. But that, she knew, was only a dream. She wouldn't dare skip any church function while living under Pa's roof.

Adele drew Elly back to the present. "Wear the pink and green cotton. It's still warm enough if you wear a wrap." She glanced at the cloudless sky. "It's going to be a beautiful day. You probably won't even need the wrap. And Gideon loves that dress."

And Bo hated it. He'd said the dress looked too babyish with its puffed sleeves and abundant ruffles, but for some reason the item still hung in her closet. The waist fit fine, but the bustline needed letting out.

"Elly?"

"Yes?"

"I should warn you that Bo will be there tonight."

"Of course. Never known a preacher to miss a free meal."

"Now you're pouting. I'll steer him clear of you, if I can."

"I can take care of myself." Elly paused and leaned on the hoe, glancing hopefully to the sky for some sign of a good hard rainstorm. That would put an end to the church supper. But nothing but a swath of blue filled her gaze.

Adele grinned. "Wear the pink and green dress tonight."

"I just might."

No, she *would*.

Especially if Pastor Bo was coming.

The air lightened as the sun sank to the west, but the day's heat released the scent of earth and hay and goodness. As the evening darkened, the sky drooped with the weight of the stars. Only the nagging insects made the night less than perfect.

Elly shook her hand to shoo the flies as she cut another fat slice of watermelon.

"Thank you, darlin'." Hank Freeman grabbed his third piece with sticky fingers. Fried chicken, pots of chicken and dumplings, golden ears of corn, green beans, and sliced tomatoes filled platters on the long row of tables. The abundant array of cakes and pies sat untouched for now, but the ripe melons kept people returning for more.

Elly focused on her task, keenly aware that Bo and his family had finally arrived. Milt and Faye found their seats quickly. The senior Garrett must have put in a long day in the bogs. His shoulders sagged with exhaustion and his color didn't seem right.

Bo walked among the church folks, holding a heaping plate of chicken, pausing occasionally to visit. His distinct laugh, deep and resonant, floated above the crowd. Berrytop welcomed him back with no questions.

Seven years had done nothing but improve his looks. His

strawberry-blond hair had darkened to a warm, sun-streaked honey. His face had filled out and his eyes had deepened, and his figure had become stronger, more muscular. He was no longer a boy.

She was so engrossed in her thoughts that she didn't hear Gideon approach.

"Hello, pretty girl." She felt the heat of his breath on her ear.

She glanced up, flashing a smile. "Hi. Ready for some melon?" She stumbled over her words, thanks to Bo. She chastised herself for her wayward thoughts and fixed her attention on Gideon. The sight of him didn't cause fireworks, but she knew she could trust him with her heart. That should be enough for any woman.

"I'm not here for watermelon. I want my girl." He took the knife from her hand and set it aside. "You've cut your share of melon. Let's go for a walk. The moon will be up soon."

Untying her apron, she handed the knife to Mary Lou Gibbons and reached for his extended hand. Gideon was a looker too, with nearly black hair, a broad, sturdy chest, and arms darkened by long hours in the sun. He was a cattleman, like his father and grandfather before him. The local flour mill took all the wheat he could grow, and he grew plenty on his two-hundred acres. Plus he had the best herd of cattle around.

Gideon was the town's catch now, and Elly should have her head examined for walking away from him. Neither she nor Gideon was getting any younger, and it wasn't a secret that he was anxious to start a family.

When the couple strolled by the Garretts, Elly nodded a greeting. Weariness seeped through Milt's voice tonight. "Elly, you're looking pretty as a picture."

Smiling, she acknowledged his compliment. She and Milt had always gotten along well. She loved the mild-mannered, jovial man who had fathered Bo. His mother, Faye, could be a bit overwhelming at times, fussing over her family like a hen with her brood, but she and Elly had never had a bad word. She refused to let her ill feelings for Bo—often confused and unruly—come between her and these fine people.

"It's a pretty night," Gideon said to the Garretts. "Air's finally cooling off a bit."

"Sure is," Faye agreed. "And I couldn't be happier." She wiped her forehead with a hanky.

Gideon steered Elly toward the river path. A light breeze ruffled her hair when the water came in sight. The moon laid a ribbon of light on the black ripples. Holding hands and feeling the warmth of him beside her, peacefulness overtook her. The couple meandered down the winding trail that lay all but invisible in the overgrowth.

"You haven't worn that dress in a while," he remarked. "I've always liked it."

Elly glanced down at the girlish pink-and-green-checked gown, faded now from so many washings. She should have chosen a newer garment, but the worn cotton proved comfortable in the mild evening. "It's old and should go in the rag bag."

"I like it. The green brings out your eyes."

Bo had said the color of the gown made her look sick.

"How's your aunt?" Gideon's thoughtfulness caught her off-guard. Would Bo even notice that Ma wasn't present at the social or remember she had gone to nurse her aunt? Surely Adele had told him.

"Doing well. Mother thinks she'll be able to come home in a few weeks. We're hoping she'll be back sooner since it's harvest time. Pa and I miss her."

"You miss her cooking," he teased.

"That too." She laughed, aware of her reputation as a woman who could burn water. Cooking took a special knack, one she didn't possess. "But I'm getting better. I didn't scorch the beans last night." Bo had often wondered out loud about the way she could take a perfectly good piece of meat and ruin it.

Why was she thinking of Bo when she walked hand-in-hand with a man who paid attention to her and her family, who had actually stuck around to build his farm, who offered his heart and his home to her?

Gideon leaned to give her a brief kiss. He had soft lips, but he kissed her like a brother. That would surely change once they were married. Kisses would be vibrant, exciting...chills would race up her arms...She caught back her thoughts before she could think, *Like it was with Bo*.

"I think you're a fine cook."

She tried to read his expression in the moonlight. "You shouldn't fib."

"Your cooking is digestible," he amended. "You haven't made me sick yet."

He knew how to add just the right amount of teasing into his tone so she didn't haul off and slug him. "Just wait. It's possible you'll change your mind."

The rising moon illuminated his face enough to reveal a sobriety that contradicted his words. She wished she'd chosen her remarks more carefully.

"I'm trying my best, Elly." His earnestness touched her. He was trying so hard to reach her.

"I know." She tugged on his arm to walk along the riverbank. How she wished she could return his feelings. He was a steady, sincere man, and most women would be eager to share his life. His next words surprised her.

"You haven't said a word about Bo."

"Bo? What about him?" She kept her tone light, although a

familiar heaviness pressed her chest at the mention of his name. She had steered clear of the subject during the walk because she didn't want to ruin the occasion with her confused feelings. Gideon paused and Elly turned to face him. The air turned thick. Flies buzzed around her. She wasn't prepared to explain her anger and attraction to Bo with this tenderhearted man. She didn't fully understand the emotions that would not let up or memories that would not release her.

For a long moment he appeared to inventory his words. "Does Bo's return make a difference in our relationship?"

She turned from him to frown at the ripples of water at her feet. "Why would you ask such a question? Bo's return doesn't make one bit of difference."

"But you're still in love with the man."

"That's ancient history. We've talked about this."

"But I still see that look in your eyes, Elly—the one you try so hard to deny. But something deep inside you won't permit it. You're still in love with Bo."

Gideon's words seem presumptuous. What was a look? One simple, impartial glance? "Nonsense. You're putting words in my mouth. I may have thought I loved him all those years ago, but when he never came back I put aside childish affections. Whatever has brought him back now, he'll be gone in a few days."

"I hear he's a pastor now."

She shrugged. "So I hear. What of it? It's cattle farmers who interest me."

Her words reassured Gideon enough to release the tension between them. "You like farmers, huh? Well, young lady, I happen to know one who's crazy about you. And that farmer—yours truly—can finally allow himself to hope for a future with you, seeing how you don't care much for preachers." He snickered. Snickered! "Don't take me wrong, Elly. It's just that I can't picture you as a preacher's wife."

For the briefest of moments she took offense at the words. She wasn't a heathen. She might doubt God's purposes, even argue with Him about why He dished out suffering to folks—letting babies die, folks get sick, crops fail. She'd seen good, kind friends who had grieved terribly. Why, Allen Bachmeier lost his arm in a wood-cutting accident, and not long after, his young wife got sick and died, leaving Allen to raise their six-month-old twin boys. And only one arm to do it.

Only the God Richardson worshipped would allow such things to happen.

Gideon's hand tightened on hers. "I don't question that you care for me, but when will affection turn to love—enough love to convince you to marry me? I'm not getting any younger, Elly, and I want children before I'm too old to enjoy them."

"You talk as though you're ancient."

"I'm nearly twenty-five, and you're not far behind me. This is our time. There's nothing to hold us back from marrying tomorrow morning, if you'd agree."

These conversations were getting more intense and frequent. How much longer could she hold back?

The answer was clear and cutting. Until she fell as deeply in love with this man as she had once loved Bo, she couldn't marry Gideon.

Elly turned toward the trail leading to the social. She stopped long enough to whisper, "I'm not ready," before she continued walking.

When he caught up to her, he took her hand. He smelled of fresh soap and a hint of lemon mingled with the scent of drying fields. Bo had distracted her, but she wouldn't let his sudden appearance upend her future. She lifted herself up on tiptoes and kissed her cattle farmer. This time, he responded with warmth that heated her stomach. She wasn't sure what to think of the reaction, but the awakening sensation brought hope. Breaking the embrace, she took his hand and continued the walk.

"If we hurry, we might see deer grazing in the meadow."

"There's no hurry, is there?"

"Pa will be looking for me. We should get back."

Gideon deserved more than she was giving. He deserved answers. But she didn't have any—and she wouldn't until Bo climbed onto his horse and rode out of town.

Until then, she remained in a dark corridor, wondering when the sun would shine again.

Chapter 4

Moonlight cast her shadow across the front porch when Elly returned home. Remnants of summer honeysuckle trailed up the railing, no longer perfuming the air. The walk had cleared her head a bit. Gideon provided good company; took her mind off cranberries and childhood crushes. The tension in her neck slowly started to release.

Reaching for the lantern Pa kept lit until she was safely in the house, she felt the tiny hairs on her arm stand up when she heard that voice, deeper now and more masculine.

"I don't believe we've said a proper hello, Miss Sullivan."

Closing her eyes, she fought back swift tears. The sound of Bo's voice was so unexpected, so welcome. The admission alarmed her. Had she been waiting for a private moment to talk to him? Certainly she'd been dreading another encounter.

Summoning an even tone, she said, "Hello, Bo."

He stepped from the shadows, leaner than she remembered. More muscled. More man. Gone was the lanky boy she had fallen head over heels in love with. In that boy's place stood the best-looking stranger she'd ever laid eyes on.

A booted foot appeared beside her dew-soaked slipper, and she tensed when his smell—rawhide and soap—washed over her. A man of the cloth should neither look nor smell so inviting. Girlish butterflies swarmed in her stomach, and she mentally netted the juvenile reaction. Silence stretched while she gathered her thoughts and summoned enough courage to face him.

"What brings you back to Berrytop?" she said, as nonchalant as a Monday morning.

His gaze skimmed her lightly, lingering on the dress. "I've seen that dress in my dreams a million times. You look prettier than ever wearing it."

She fixed him with a cold stare. "You hated this dress. Besides, the garment's seven years older than when you last saw it. I wore it for Gideon."

"Gideon is a blessed man."

Finding her pride, she pushed past him and was about to open the door when he put his hand above the sill, momentarily trapping her. His nearness nearly undid her. "We need to talk." His breath softly brushed her cheek. For a moment the world tilted. She would not treat this man as though he were the old Bo. She would *not*.

She turned and crossed her arms. "What do you want, Bo?" She'd known this hour would come—dreaded it, longed for it, despaired of it. He could still turn her insides to pulp.

"Could we sit for a moment?"

At his gentle invitation, a flame ignited her anger. "Weren't you supposed to be back in—oh—two to three months, at the most? What happened? Did you get lost? Didn't you have the money for a horse or a train ticket?" She snatched the lantern off the hook. "A simple wire. You could have at the very least sent word that you were still alive."

"Hold on, give me a minute. You have every right to your anger. Can we sit in the swing and talk? I promise not to keep you long."

The swing had been their place to sit and talk under her parents' watchful eyes. The thought of sitting there with him now made her blood boil. "Absolutely not, Bo." She shooed away a pesky fly. "Drat these bothersome pests."

"You're going to make this even worse, are you?" He took her by the hand, pulled her off the porch and toward the swing that hung from the oak. "Have a heart, lady. I'm only asking for a couple of minutes."

"I'm clean out of minutes. I used them all waiting for you to return."

Half dragging her to the swing, he settled into the weathered wood and she wondered if she had lost her mind. She'd had no intention of ever speaking to this man again, and now she was sitting in the swing, the place of stolen kisses, soft whispers, and empty promises.

She jerked her hand from his. They sat in stony silence with only night birds for company.

Finally, he began. "Reverend Richardson preached often on the ease of slipping from the righteous path. I thought it was all talk—that Richardson just liked to yell. But there is great truth in what he preached."

Elly covered her ears, trying to block the words, shield them from penetrating her heart.

He calmly reached over and pulled her hands off her ears. "Stop it, Elly. You have to hear this, like it or not."

"You always believed Richardson when we were young." She vividly recalled the wintery afternoon they'd carved their initials in the tree and discussed their beliefs. He had been the stronger one.

"I did—until I left home. After that, lines started to blur." He loosened his collar.

She winced when she felt his thigh touch hers—an innocent gesture, but the touch felt like a hot poker. The swing was barely big enough to hold two adults. Naturally they would make contact. She scooted until the wooden arm pinched her in the ribs.

For a long time he leaned back, closed his eyes, and appeared to be sorting through the years. Or was he simply absorbing the feel of home? Sitting here, like this, made events of the past seven years fade away. This was Bo and Elly, two people who vowed nothing could ever separate them.

She finally broke the silence. "I don't know where you've been or what you've done, but what we once had is over."

"I'm aware of that."

"Then why are you here?"

"I owe you an explanation."

"Nothing you could think up would appease me, Bo. You must know that."

"I'm not trying to pacify you. I want to tell you my side of the story and then I'll leave, Elly. You have my word."

She threw her hands up. "Why now? Why come home now? When seven years passed without a word from you, I assumed the earth had devoured you. You were either dead or you'd married someone else and didn't bother to inform me."

"I'm not married. I told you I would never marry anyone but you."

She opened her mouth, clamped it shut, and stared at him. Stars lit the cool night.

He continued, "I don't deserve a grain of kindness from you. I have wronged you, betrayed you, and broken about every promise I made to you. I know our lives will never be the same, but if you could find it in your heart to forgive me, I would greatly appreciate the effort."

Elly hadn't prepared herself to be in a forgiving mood. Maybe if she knew exactly where he'd been and why he'd stayed away so long, she might be able to give the matter some thought.

"So?"

"So, I've been driving cattle, mostly. Fell in with a rowdy bunch. We frequented saloons, drank until sunup, and rode herd with a hangover in order to buy more liquor."

With each word her heart sank. This was not conduct she could forgive—even for a man she loved more than life.

"It took a lightning bolt to my head to make me realize I was wasting my life. I nearly died." He paused. "Is this what you wanted to hear?"

It was not what she wanted to hear. She would never have guessed the story could be so painful to listen to. "It took you a good long time to find your roots."

How easy it would be to buy what he was selling, to grasp the side of his lifeboat. He had wanted a life of adventure and had finally decided to settle down. Every young man did to one extent or another, but not Bo—her Bo. His roots were firmly planted in the cranberry bogs of Wisconsin, with her. At least, they should have been.

"I missed home. You, Ma, Pa, Anne, Adele. Even ol' Reverend Righteous. I figured you'd all got on with your lives while I was mired in sin. Shame nearly sucked the life out of me. The thought of facing you and the family, telling everyone where I'd been and about the life I'd lived, kept me away. The past couple of years Ma knew how to get in touch with me."

"I know." The thought ate away at Elly. He no longer loved her enough to even allow Faye to tell her of his whereabouts. Faye had watched the way Elly grieved—always wondering, constantly watching the roads. Elly wouldn't have been shocked to see someone bring his dead body strapped to the back of his horse to Berrytop for burial. Never once had she thought he'd been living an immoral life.

The two sat in silence as she tried to absorb his words. Perhaps somewhere in her heart she had been waiting for a miracle. That hope had just been taken away. He hadn't mentioned other women, but the subject followed the lifestyle he'd lived. At least he'd spared her that image.

She fumbled for a hanky in her dress pocket to wipe her eyes. "What changed? You're here now."

"My love for Ma and Pa outpaced my shame. I joined a church, took up with a pastor who eventually became my best friend, and what you have sitting here is the new Bo Garrett."

Her eyes lightly skimmed his worn denims and work shirt. He'd certainly changed in appearance, but in most ways he was still the same old Bo. She couldn't imagine her Bo living the life he'd described. She shook her head, the fight draining out of her. There was a time to hold on and a time to let go, and she finally understood that this was her time to let go. "I don't know what to say, Bo."

"If you'll forgive me, Elly, that will be enough. And I'd like to be friends, if that's possible. I know I've let you down, but there's not one thing I can do to change my past."

Friends? He wanted to resume a *friendship*? If she said no it would be like refusing God a favor. "Of course, Bo. We've always been...friends." She located the hanky and wiped her nose.

He smiled and gently reached to pat her hand. Like a brother. Or a kind stranger. "To tell you the truth, I'm not sure what the future holds. I have a congregation back in Parsons, Kansas, but Ma needs me here. Pa's real sick, Elly. His heart's failing. Right now I plan to

stay through the harvest and then return to Parsons. By then I hope
he'll have improved. While I'm here, I don't want us avoiding each
other, crossing the street when we spot each other coming, living in
cold silence. That's not the kind of people we are."

His words were ebbing and flowing in giant waves. He'd lived an
immoral life. Milt was gravely ill. Most likely there had been other
women in his life…

Milt Garrett hadn't looked like himself in some time. Faye
always offered an excuse for her husband's noticeable change. He'd
worked harder than usual. He caught a cold. He lay awake worrying about Bo.

"How long has Milt been sick?"

Bo shook his head. "His heart's been increasingly worse over the
years. Doc told Ma he didn't have much longer, but Doc isn't God.
He may have years—and it could be today." He sat up to face her. "I
hear you nearly married last year." Pain lay deep in his eyes, but the
sincerity in his voice was evident. "You should marry Gideon, start
a family, live your life to the fullest." The grin that never failed to
twist her heart surfaced, tugging at her resolve. "I'm only asking for
your forgiveness. I understand there are some things a woman can
never forgive, and I've done all of them, Elly."

Her gaze traced the outline of his familiar features, slightly older
and more careworn than she remembered. He couldn't have hurt
her more profoundly than if he'd shoved a knife through her heart.
Could she ever really forgive him?

It was a good thing he wasn't asking for more than friendship.

He had been the boy she loved. He had been her best friend on
earth, and the sweet memories of long-ago days with him reminded
her of who he was and who she was, and neither would ever be the
same again.

"I forgive you, Bo." She wished she could offer a little more enthusiasm, but he was lucky she was still speaking. He'd filled in more blanks than she wanted to hear.

"That's my girl," he said softly. "I've set out to serve the Lord with all my might, Elly. I haven't forgotten how you feel about preachers and the promise I made you, but when God takes hold of a man's will and breaks it, He's impossible to refuse." He extended his hand. "Friends?"

She slowly laid her hand in his, and he held it tight.

"I'll be going now," he said. "You need your rest."

"No," she found herself saying. "Stay awhile."

She felt as though she'd been at war for seven years and she'd finally seen the white flag of surrender. Maybe now she could finally release her heart to another man.

"All right. Tell me about you and Gideon," he said. "What made you back out of marrying him?"

"I didn't back out. I needed more time to plan the wedding. When a girl changes her whole life, she needs time to get organized."

"Organized? Like clean house, cook meals ahead, spruce up the yard, cut a few tree limbs, that sort of thing?"

"Of course not." He could always ruffle her practical side and shred good old everyday sense.

"Sounds like a pitiful excuse to me."

Sighing, she realized that if they were going to be friends he would know her every thought. He always had—and usually before she thought it. He had an uncanny way of reading her mind, but telling him she couldn't marry Gideon because she'd been waiting for him seemed like a betrayal not only to her but to Gideon. "I wasn't ready for marriage."

"Marriage is a big commitment."

The years fell away as they talked. And talked. And the stars shone all the brighter as the brief hours passed.

She finally stood up. "Dawn will be here soon, and harvest is starting."

"Of course. It's late. I'm sorry."

"No. It was good." The night had been food for her starving soul. For a brief time, Bo was back in her life—not forever, but long enough for her to remember why she'd loved and protected his memory so fiercely all these long years.

He walked her to the door, where she noticed Pa had extinguished the lantern. She automatically lifted her face for Bo's kiss and stopped. Their eyes met. Startled, she stepped back.

"See you in church," he said.

She nodded. "I'll be there, preacher."

At the sight of his retreating back, her throat closed and her eyes swam with unshed tears. All these years of hoping and dreaming had come to this moment: Bo would never be hers, ever.

Her head swam with the revelations this night had brought. How Bo had lived a rough life, how he'd found a home in the church, how he'd missed her but wallowed in shame, and how he would never have come home if not for Milt's illness.

He wanted to be friends.

Now that she knew her hopes for a life with him were over, she could marry Gideon. She would make him happy.

And she would make sure he never knew she was settling.

But she'd know.

That's what bothered her; she would know. Every single day of her life she would know that she would never love another man like she had once loved Bo Garrett.

Chapter 5

The sun redoubled its efforts to parch the earth before fully surrendering to fall. Elly had spent the morning getting a start on supper for her and Pa. It had been another long week since hearing from Ma. How she wished she were here to reassure her, to remind her God had only Elly's best in mind.

Now, Elly tightened the lid on a canning jar and set the drink beside a cold biscuit filled with bacon slices in the picnic basket.

Gideon would be thrilled with the surprise. This morning she was a woman with a mission. She would fall madly in love with Gideon, no matter what it took.

It would be more difficult than she'd first thought. She'd woken to a mess of rumpled sheets from tossing and turning, willing her heart to release the final memory of Bo in her dreams. By dawn she knew she had lost the struggle but not the battle.

So Gideon would be the object of her full attention from here on out. Starting today, he was everything to her. Loving the cattle farmer should have come as easy as breathing. He deserved complete devotion and she would deliver it. He'd gone to school with her and Bo. They'd met most summer days at Pellet's pond to swing and dive into the deep pool that collected behind felled trees. From her earliest memories, he sat in a church pew—three rows down from her family. She played children's games with him and caught fireflies on warm summer nights. She thought of him as a brother...and therein lay the obstacle. He had always been more brother than deep-down soul mate.

Shaking the hesitation aside, she reflected that her life could turn out far worse married to any of the other eligible men in town. Mr. Swan was looking for a wife. His wife, Viola, had died in childbirth last year, a birth that made him father to six children. And Aaron Bristol also made it plain he was in the market for a lady. The man had roving eyes and spit when he talked. The thought of either choice chilled her to the bone. Gideon did not.

She closed the lid on the basket and glanced around the kitchen. Pa would come in from the bogs hungry and in no mood to wait for supper. She'd peeled potatoes and roasted a chicken to buy time for her brief visit with Gideon. She scribbled a quick note of explanation and left it on the table in case Pa found his way home early.

Gideon's place was a good two miles down the road. Elly counted the white faces of curious steer as she walked along his well-maintained fence line. She stopped counting at fifty. She knew he grazed many more on his two hundred acres, but if you'd seen one steer you'd seen them all.

The Long homestead lacked the female touch of the Sullivans' place. No summer petunias lined the porch. The mismatched windows tilted among the rough logs. But a sturdy rock fireplace rose above the roofline, and the outbuildings wore a fresh coat of white paint. There was no denying the practicality of her soon-to-be new home.

The Longs were known for their frugal ways. It was said Gideon's father had enough money to burn a wet mule when he passed a couple of years earlier. Shortly after his death, Gideon's mother had gone to live with her sister in California until her grief lessened. So far, she hadn't returned. Rumor had it she'd never warmed to the town of Berrytop.

Elly released a sigh of relief when she spotted Gideon repairing a harness in the shade of the barn. She wouldn't have to hunt for him along the long lines of fences.

His features lit when he recognized her.

Smiling, she covered the ground between them, swinging the basket. Where Bo's voice had rallied a swarm of insects to anguish her, the sight of Gideon didn't awaken so much as a tiny moth in her stomach. So be it. Who needed insects to enhance their love life?

Lord, Gideon is a good man who deserves a loving, devoted wife. Make me that person. Wake my heart to love him fully and completely.

Gideon rose to his feet and wiped his hands on a cloth. "What brings my best girl out on such a fine morning?" He glanced at the sun. "Guess it's closer to afternoon, isn't it?"

"I brought a bite to eat and something cool to drink." She set the basket beside him and lifted her face for his kiss, something she expected to do a million times over the coming years. Gideon hadn't shaved and his prickly beard scratched her.

"Sorry," he said, rubbing a hand over the dark stubble. "I wasn't expecting company." His gaze lit on the basket. "I could eat, though." He opened the lid. At the sight of the biscuit and bacon, he kissed her cheek. "Let's sit on the porch. A breeze comes up from the stream and it's real nice this time of day."

The predicted light wind met them on their arrival. Settled on a bench, he lifted the biscuit out of the basket. "You do know how to please a man," he said.

"I knew you wouldn't stop to eat. You never do."

He chewed thoughtfully, apparently enjoying the unexpected respite...and her company. As he ate, Elly studied his features. His lashes were long enough to paint a barn. They framed eyes nearly as black as the Wisconsin soil. A straight nose, well-proportioned, sat in the middle of his face. His lips plumped nicely and his teeth were as straight as tombstones, only whiter. And he'd always had a strong chin. Before long, this would be the first face she saw every morning and the last face she saw at night.

The future started now. "Gideon..." she began.

He raised his eyebrows, his mouth full of biscuit.

"I've been thinking," she said with as much conviction as she could muster.

He stopped chewing to muffle, "Go on."

"You're right. It's time...I think...to consider a new wedding date."

His hand lowered, leaving a flake of biscuit on his lower lip. Disbelief crossed his features. "You're sure?"

Firming her lips, she nodded. "Very sure."

Wrapping the biscuit in the napkin, he turned pensive. His reaction surprised her. She'd thought he would leap with joy. Instead, his features turned grave. He swallowed and took a deep drink of lemonade before he spoke again. "When?"

When? She wasn't prepared to set a date, merely to reopen the discussion. She needed time to give her love for Gideon a chance to grow. Perhaps mentioning the subject had been premature.

"The harvest is top priority," she said.

"Most things are more important than us marrying."

The bite of what he said startled her. "Gideon." She placed a gentle hand on his arm. It hurt her to see the truth laid bare in his eyes. "I'm not going to deny it's taken me a long time to get over Bo, but I have accepted that the man who came back is not the Bo who rode away so many years ago."

Struggle played across his features. Leaning, she gently turned his face to meet hers. "I will make you a good wife, Gideon. I will care for your needs and mother your children, and we'll live a good life. I'm sorry I made you wait so long for a second wedding date, but I had to be sure. I respect you enough to make certain I could offer you my solemn promise."

His gaze softened. "I've waited so long for this hour, Elly. And I will make you love me."

The words were so stark, and completely out of place in a wedding discussion.

"I...I love you now, Gideon." At least, she believed the seed of love had been fully planted. And that seed would grow, even more once they were married.

"I'll be good to you, Elly. And our children." He bent and kissed her, long and sweet. When he pulled back, he smiled. "You won't know what to do with all the love I give you."

Laughing, she looped her arm through his and snuggled closer, studying the fields, the fences, and the livestock that would soon be part of her life. "I know little about raising cattle, but I can bake edible cranberry muffins."

Drawing her closer, he rested his chin on the top of her head. "I love you more than five men put together."

"Better wait until you taste my muffins before you go that far." Their mouths drifted together for another long kiss. She could do this. Men were men. If she was capable of adoring Bo all these years, loving Gideon would be easy.

He set up straighter. "So when's the date?"

"Well, obviously not before Ma comes home. I suppose we can't set the final, final date, but I would guess sometime before the first of the year."

His smile faded. "This year, or next year?"

"This year, silly. Perhaps between Thanksgiving and Christmas?"

He leaned and kissed her again. Then spoke softly against her lips. "No sooner?"

The insistence in his voice made her uneasy. But she couldn't blame him for pressing. If she hadn't stopped the ceremony earlier, they'd be married by now. He loved her. He wanted to be with her. He'd more than earned her loyalty. She should be flattered. And she should be returning his love more ardently. "Soon. Before the New Year."

"Do I have your promise?"

"Wild horses couldn't stop me."

And she meant it. She was done being the source of agony in Gideon Long's life.

Long live true love.

Chapter 6

The Berrytop Ladies Quilting Society bent their heads over a lovely log cabin coverlet to be presented to Adele at the birth of her baby. Although mornings were crisp, the fall weather remained warm enough for windows to be thrown open and outdoor activities to carry on. Cramped into Widow Olsen's parlor, the women worked to the sound of people chatting as they walked along Main Street and wagons hurrying by on their way back to farms with loads of supplies from the dry goods store. Elly enjoyed what passed for hustle and bustle in Berrytop. Farm life could get awfully quiet.

Elly sat next to Cecelia Lane at the quilting frame. Cee had never been a particularly close friend, but Elly enjoyed her company. Elly couldn't deny that she was the prettiest girl in town. She'd heard many boys admire her slim figure and the lovely contrast between her dark curls and clear blue eyes. And her giving nature only added to the package.

Cee couldn't help that she was a born tease; she wore the trait well and had yet to get serious about any one man, though she was definitely husband hunting. She was a predictable member of the

Ladies Quilting Society, never missing a session. The ladies of the group envied her tidy stitches more than her eye appeal.

And anyway, her beauty could have been a point of debate that day. A nose raw from continual wiping matched her watery red eyes. Two explosive sneezes in the last five minutes encouraged the women to ease their chairs into a defensive huddle at the opposite end of the quilting frame. Cee didn't seem to notice. After yet another explosive *ah-choo!* Elly quietly suggested that she might feel better at home. In bed.

Cee stopped stitching to rest her hands on the quilt top. "Perhaps, but the distraction of your company probably helps more." She picked her needle up again and gathered perfectly spaced stitches. "Is the Reverend still planning another social for Sunday evening?" Her needle paused. Women lifted their heads, expectantly. A clutched hanky flew to Cee's mouth before a sneeze escaped. "Drat! I detest this time of year. It's something to do with the hay cutting, I know it." She sneezed twice more.

Cee welcomed the church socials. Why not? She was the center of attention, although Elly couldn't say that the young woman ever let her looks go to her head. She wasn't a snob. She'd been nothing but nice, truly pleasant company. And, most important in a farming community, Cee worked as hard as anyone in the bogs.

Elly, on the other hand, missed a stitch over the thought of another ice cream social. Preparations for harvest filled her days. All she cared for by sundown was a cold meal and a soft bed. Only putting the final touches on Adele's baby quilt had given her reason to be at quilting circle. There would be extra work to do when she got home. And now Reverend Righteous's sweet tooth meant more baking and fuss—at a time when the community could ill afford to spare the time.

"Nickolas and Saul made sure the ice house was full," said Laura

Mae Bacon, a white-haired lady who never tired of parties and socials. "Near broke their backs, but they're boasting of how many bowls of ice cream the Reverend can eat this week."

Surely not enough to freeze his acid tongue. Elly shook the uncharitable thought from her head. Just because she didn't care for the preacher's way of presenting the gospel didn't mean he wasn't a virtuous man. He was. He rushed to comfort the bedridden, never missed a congregational birthday or anniversary celebration, and made sure his assembly gathered for regular events. She should be kinder in her thoughts.

"The ice house is full of strawberries and peaches," Laura Mae's sister, Sally Anne, added. Laura Mae always stayed after the other quilters had left to take out Sally Anne's irregular stitches and replace them with her own. "We had a good yield this year. I put aside plenty for the social."

Another violent sneeze rocked the room. Cee wiped her nose and said in a nasal whisper, "Mother has been rationing sugar, so there'll be plenty. After running low last year, she swore she'd never put herself in the position of relying on the sweetness of the fruit and honey to appease everyone."

A breeze lifted a window curtain. Elly's eyes strayed to the outside, and she spotted Bo walking into the feed store. It was impossible to avoid him in this small town. He'd been home a week and townsfolk still expected the two of them to take up where they'd left off. They would be waiting a long time.

As much as she fought the impulse, every glimpse of his tall, sturdy frame caused a spark of excitement, the feeling she got when a lightning bolt struck nearby. Today his face was lined with worry, as if he carried the heavy burden of his father's illness. Her eyes fastened on him as he opened the screen door and stepped inside the granary.

One of the women also spotted him. "It's so good to see Bo back home. Imagine, our boy is a preacher! And a right fine one, I hear."

Pleased murmurs floated around the table.

"His ma seems relieved to have him stay on." A needle paused in midair. "Has anyone else noticed the heavy circles under Milt's eyes? I asked if he was feeling poorly, but he said he was fit as a fiddle."

Sally Anne nodded. "He doesn't seem himself lately. Why, I saw him sitting down beside a bog right in the middle of the day, and I've never seen that man take a break. Not ever. I bet Bo's staying on because his pa is ill."

Elly bit off a thread. Milt was a sick man, but she'd given her promise to keep the fact quiet. He might look a bit puny, but knowing Milt, he would be his old self before long. Doctors couldn't say how long a man lived; Milt would fool them all.

Irene Shuster, the resident know-it-all, shook her head. "I don't think that's why he's here. It's only logical he'd want to spend time with his folks. And why wouldn't he? He's been away so long. Adele told me everything is fine, and she'd be the first to say otherwise if something was amiss." Irene huffed with self-satisfaction over her apparent inside knowledge of the Garrett family. She needed something to give her satisfaction—heaven knew her stitches were nothing to brag about.

"That would be decent of him," Elly murmured.

Irene glanced up. "Did you say something, dear?"

Elly sucked on her finger. "No. I pricked myself. It's a shame Adele can't be here today. She would love to work on the quilt. She's awfully uncomfortable. Pregnancy's been hard on her. And losing Ike. Especially losing Ike."

Irene peered at Elly over her glasses, tsking. "Such a dear, sweet man, Ike. You and Bo were a couple for a very long time, weren't you, lovey? I recall telling my husband when you'd see one the other would be along shortly." She smiled as if she'd caught Elly with her hand in the cookie jar. "My, how our lives and intentions change as we get older. Why, I hear tell that Bo—he turned downright shameful once he left home. Don't know what happened, but he seems like a good man now. Fairly bursting with the Lord."

Mustering a smile, Elly conceded. "Life is full of surprises."

Several chuckles followed the comment and the stories started. "Why, I recall the day you and Bo got into Henry Dunkle's orchard. It was on a Saturday. The two of you ate a bushel of green apples. The next morning, you and Bo kept the church's front door flapping, running out to the privy. I thought Reverend was going to come unhinged."

"As well as your father," Laura Mae teased.

Nodding, Elly tried to change the subject. "Can someone show me how to tie off the thread? I keep forgetting the new technique Imogene taught us."

Imogene leaned over the frame and demonstrated how to pull the knot through the fabric. If Elly thought asking for help would turn the ladies from discussing her and Bo, she was wrong.

Imogene chuckled. "Do you remember the time Elly and Bo painted that mutt red?"

The room erupted in laughter.

"Didn't hurt the dog, but I bet your backside stung for a few days, huh, Elly?" That from Cee, which stung a little.

Elly nodded, still recalling the pain. When Pa meted out punishment, it wasn't pleasant. A good strong willow switch convinced her to leave the dog alone and to accept its ugly markings. Bo's parents merely laughed at the prank. Milt confessed he'd even considered doing something to help the poor animal.

Agatha Paisley looked up from her stitching and pinched her black eyes in Elly's direction. "At least those were harmless pranks.

You hooligans tied war bonnet feathers on all the hogs' heads. They looked like a bunch of wild Indians running around the pen."

"But we didn't hurt anything," Elly pointed out.

"The dickens you didn't! Those hogs didn't settle down for days. Never thought the meat tasted quite right, neither."

Tears smarted to Elly's eyes at the unwelcomed memories. The women thought the incidents amusing, but the subject only reminded her of what she'd lost. She fumbled for a hanky.

"Oh dear, I hope you're not coming down with Cee's cold," Laura Mae said.

Cee sneezed on cue. "It's the hay, I tell you."

Elly dabbed at her eyes. "I'm fine. It's that time of year." Or the thought of innocent youth, days when God's good will shone on her. Those days were far gone.

"You know, dear, there's another couple here in town that reminds me of you and Bo when you were young'uns."

"Who might that be, Mrs. Oke?"

"Young Rosie and Quint. Other than you and Bo, I've never seen a couple more suited for each other."

"Just the other day I was thinking the same, Prudence. Like Bo and Elly, where you see one you see the other."

"Humph." Laura Mae glanced up. "Those silly young'uns don't have one good brain between 'em. Quint ran down one of our mules last week and was ridin' the silly thing at breakneck speed to impress Rosie, I assume. He was so engrossed in his tomfoolery he rode straight into a tree branch and near knocked his brains out. Later I heard his ma dusted his backside with a thick switch. He knows he's not supposed to be ridin' our animals."

"They're only children, Laura Mae."

"Children my foot. Quint's been taught better." The older woman sniffed. "And so has Rosie."

"I think they're adorable," Cee said. "The way they follow each other around like puppy dogs—it's cute." She sighed. "Come to think of it, Elly, they *are* exactly like you and Bo were at their age."

Elly carefully thread a needle. "I hope Rosie doesn't really believe Quint will feel the same about her when he's old enough to marry." The bitter reflection slipped out before Elly could catch it. Heads lifted. Eyes peered in her direction.

"What I meant to say is, they are young and life has a way of playing tricks on us."

Imogene leaned in and patted her hand. "How is Gideon? Such a fine, upstanding man. You are indeed blessed, Elly, to have his attention. Is there a new wedding date?"

Imogene knew better. News like that would have spread like hot butter. When Elly delayed the first wedding date, the town knew every detail before she walked home to tell her parents.

Sally Anne added, "Yes, honey, you mustn't keep Gideon waiting forever."

Cee caught Elly's eye, probably seeing her distress. She jumped in to change the subject, holding up a piece of green thread. "Is this the right color?"

Once the quilters recovered from the horror of Cee's thread choice, conversations drifted to other topics: the latest cranberry prices, preparations for the coming winter, their next quilting project. In the backs of everyone's minds was the isolation winter brought to northern Wisconsin.

Harvest would come and go, and all eyes would study the sky for the first snow. Winter meant settling into cocoons to find the warmth of a fire, family, and the quilts they stitched.

Later that morning, Elly and Cee walked home with their sewing kits over their arms. The bright sunshine overhead made thoughts of the approaching winter even less tolerable. The women's slippers kicked up soft puffs in the dusty road. The bogs lay ahead of them, a sight to behold with the berries deepening to a crimson red.

"Thank you for changing the subject today," Elly said.

"About Gideon?"

"About Bo."

"Oh, that. You were squirming. I feared you'd run out of the parlor screaming if I didn't say something." Cee glanced at her. "You're still stuck on him, aren't you?"

"Absolutely not." She wasn't *stuck*. She could move on whenever she wanted. "I detest the community whispering behind my back."

"This town loves to whisper, that's for sure. They wonder what could have made Bo leave and not come back for so long. I supposed the two of you broke up before he left?"

Apparently they had, only he hadn't told her. They had spoken of marriage and babies right up to the moment Bo informed her he wanted to see some of the world before he settled down. He was restless—inquisitive about what lay beyond Berrytop and Madison's boundaries. Talk about the Wild West, tall mountain ranges, and Kansas wheat fields suddenly captivated him. Elly could see excitement build in his eyes when the old timers talked about their youthful escapades.

"I'll make a better husband and pa if I know a little about the world, Elly."

His desire to explore hadn't surprised or concerned her. She was so smug, so confident in their future that she never dreamed he'd be gone over a month.

She never once considered he'd be gone for seven long years, or that he would be a different man when he finally came back.

Yet she was relieved to have someone to talk to about Bo. With Ma gone and Adele easily upset, she'd harbored her thoughts about him in silence. Adele would soon be consumed with care for her infant. With all the changes taking place, Elly welcomed a chance to grow closer to Cee.

She eased to the road's edge behind Cee when she heard a wagon approaching from behind. The driver pulled up on the reins to stop. Bo tipped his hat from his place on the bench. He looked her straight in the eye and bid her a good afternoon, but it was Cee who jumped to acknowledge his greeting.

"Morning, Bo. Lovely day!" she chirped.

"One of God's finest!" His gaze remained fastened on Elly. "Better put your bonnet on, Miss Elly. You know how you freckle in the sun." Whistling, he smacked the reins against the horse's rump and the buckboard rattled on.

Both girls waved away the dust. The wagon clambered up a modest hill and sank into the depression beyond, disappearing from sight.

Cee sneezed into her hanky. "You do realize how blessed you were to ever have a man like Bo in love with you? He could have chosen any girl in town before he left."

Was that envy in Cee's tone? The recognition startled her. Cee and Bo? She'd never imagined the pairing. But she should have. Cee was pretty and talented enough to attract a man like Bo. And while she teased along with others about Pastor Richardson's fiery tongue, the young woman was upright and a strong believer.

Elly bit her lower lip in concentration. Cee was lovely, but she could be a bit spoiled, even temperamental at times. However, she had seen her blush over her self-indulgence and step out of the limelight to turn her attention to her parents, or an elderly person sitting by herself. That made her warm and lovable. Elly realized she'd been wearing her love—or was it simple infatuation?—for Bo like a restricting corset. She could barely breathe or think. Those ties were loosening as she looked at Cee with new eyes. If she couldn't have Bo, the least she could do was pair him with a good woman. Cee would make an excellent pastor's wife. Warm. Caring.

"I didn't know you admired Bo," Elly said, meaning to test the waters of Cee's affections.

Her friend lifted a shoulder. "Don't be offended, but yes, it's difficult not to be attracted to such a man. And now that he's in the ministry, well..." She swiped at the dust on her skirt. "I've dreamed of being a pastor's wife. And Bo is special. I would be honored—thrilled—to catch his eye." Cee's hand flew to her mouth, her eyes wide with astonishment. Clearly she'd said more than she'd intended. "Oh, Elly! I'm sorry. I know how you feel about him."

"Please." Elly held up a hand. "How I feel about him—or once felt about him—no longer matters. Youthful crushes are over."

"You've said this before, but is it true?" Her eyes searched Elly's. "Are you sure you no longer have feelings for him?"

Elly wasn't certain about anything but one fact: She would never marry a pastor. And Bo had chosen to serve his angry God over loving her.

He wanted to be friends.

And she wanted her old Bo back.

"He isn't mine to hand over. And you don't need my permission to—"

To what? To court him? To marry him? The words settled over her heart like a wool blanket. Fortunately, Bo and Cee wouldn't live in Berrytop, right under her nose for the rest of her life. Once Milt felt better, Bo would return to Parsons and his congregation, maybe bringing a brand new wife with him.

Maybe Cee would have the honor of being called Mrs. Bo Garrett. Pastor Garrett's wife. Mother of Pastor Garrett's children.

And when Bo was gone, she could easily lay any lingering thoughts of him to rest.

"To?" Cee prompted.

Elly shifted her sewing kit and swallowed dust. "To do anything you like. Gideon and I will be marrying soon."

"Oh, goodness!" Relief escaped Cee with a whoosh. Apparently she'd given the idea of marriage and Bo considerable thought. "I'm so happy you're accepting of the situation."

Accepting? Elly hardly thought surrender could be considered acceptance, but she was beaten.

Silence fell between the two women when a second buckboard passed. Once the clatter died away, Cee continued. "Isn't it wonderful how God works? Here I've been wondering how I might approach you about the subject, and He makes talking to you as easy as the wheat bending in the breeze."

Cee kept simplifying the matter, like going to the store to purchase a tin of fruit. Giving Bo to another woman was much more complicated.

The Sullivan house came into view. The old homestead lent a particular welcoming feel today, sheltering. If Ma had been here, Elly would have found a cup of hot tea waiting, the scent of supper sizzling on the woodstove, and most lovely of all, her mother's generous love. She would pull a chair up to the table and they would talk. She would make Elly see that she and Bo were no longer suited for each other. It was time to put away childish whims and look to the future, a future that now seemed certain with Gideon. All Elly had to do was set the wedding date and her worries would be behind her.

The two women paused at the front gate. Cee sought Elly's gaze. "Bo's never given me a second glance. I'm just wishing."

Forcing an agreeable smile, Elly thought, *Why not?* If she couldn't have Bo, Cee could. He couldn't know what she was doing; he would bull up and tell her to mind her own business. Still, she couldn't stand the thought of his marrying someone completely unsuited for him. Obviously, the man could be fooled by a pretty smile.

Bo wasn't a side of beef hanging in Mr. Stack's mercantile, and more to the point, he wasn't hers to give away, but Cee wouldn't hurt him. She would make a doting wife, and together their love would create beautiful children. Tears swelled to her eyes and she averted her gaze. "I must be running along. Father likes dinner on time."

Squeezing Elly's hand, Cee smiled. "It's been fun. We must take more walks together."

Nodding, Elly returned her smile. "We must."

She would give Cee twenty-four hours before she had a steaming dish on Bo's doorstep.

After all, she only had a short time to win the preacher's heart; harvest would be over by early November and Bo would most likely leave. He wasn't blind. If a girl like Cee sought his attention, he would be attracted like any other man. That meant long walks, where Cee would prattle away about the details of her budding romance with Bo....

"Have a marvelous afternoon." Cee hurried off, humming under her breath, no doubt planning a chicken dish to bait the snare.

Elly Sullivan. What have you done?

Warm days gradually cooled. October arrived, turning the birches, oaks, and maples into bright yellows, warm golds, and blazing reds. Harvest was well underway. Elly studied this year's crop, which looked to be even more plentiful. Bouquets of vibrant berries nestled in crate after crate. Her heart warmed at the hardy berries' determination to produce so generously.

The cloth-covered basket of fresh blueberry muffins felt light in her hands this morning. Hearing the ladies of the quilting society speak of Milt Garrett's failing health had motivated her to try her hand at baking. Again.

Unlatching the gate, she stepped inside the yard, using the heel of her boot to kick the latch closed. Bo had been so busy in the bogs that she rarely saw him these days, and she was thankful. She didn't count the times she stood at the window and spied on him while he worked in a front bog, picking and crating the berries. Other than the conversation they'd had in the swing and brief nods with few words, she and Bo carefully avoided each other. The past was clearly the past.

Adele greeted her warmly. "I smell muffins, don't I?" Her middle swelled more each day as her baby grew. By the time the child arrived in late December, Adele would be waddling like a duck.

Elly lifted the cloth to confirm her friend's suspicions. "They're for your father."

"Wonderful! He shares, but Bo doesn't so don't let him see them." The two women embraced. "This is so thoughtful of you."

She affectionately patted her friend's expanding waistline. "I hope the baby likes blueberries."

"He or she adores them." Adele flashed an impish grin. "These cooler days make me feel less like a sausage busting out of its casing."

It was so good to hear life back in her friend's voice. Adele still had days of weeping and sorrow. When last they'd spoken, Adele announced that her husband's death to be "God's will." Such a pronouncement confused Elly. Why would God need Ike Frost? Adele needed him here, especially with his child on its way.

"I'm glad you're comfortable," Elly said.

"I didn't say I was comfortable. It's just so lovely this time of year that it's hard to feel bad."

Most folks considered the brilliantly colored bog and the cooler days as markers for the beginning of a long hard winter. Adele's optimism said even more about her sunny outlook.

Elly's gaze swept the empty kitchen. "Where's Faye?"

"She took Pa to town. She wants the doc to give him a tonic." Her friend's features turned pensive as she absently rubbed her rounded belly. "He doesn't seem himself. I can't get Bo to say a thing about Pa's health, but I think something is wrong. I'd say he's overworked, but he always works hard during harvest season."

Three weeks ago, the pickers had wrapped their fingers in strips of cloth to protect themselves from the plants' prickles and set to work. Elly's father, considered progressive, now used wooden, hand-held scoops to comb the berries from the plants, which helped some. All pickers were overworked, young or old. But not many cranberry farmers stopped long enough to take trips to the doctor during harvest.

Adele shook her head as if to dismiss concern. "Doc will give him something to perk him up. I'll make us a pot of tea, and then we'll split one of your muffins."

Elly grinned. "I brought extra."

Adele turned, pretending surprise. "You did?"

Elly swatted her with the cloth she'd slipped off the basket. "One for you; one for the baby."

Her friend poured steaming water into the porcelain teapot. "Are you suggesting I'm a glutton?"

"Never. The baby's a hog."

Adele plumped a pillow and moved to sit down when a ruckus erupted outside. She hoisted herself up to step to the window. "What in the world...?"

Elly pushed back her chair and rose to join her. "What is it?"

"I'm not certain. Did you buy some cattle?"

"Cattle?" She stood behind Adele at the window, peering over her shoulder. Gideon and one of his farmhands herded two steers, both good size, up the lane to the Sullivan farm.

Turning on her heel, Elly raced outside toward her house, waving her arms. "Gideon! Hello!"

The farmer turned, a smile breaking across his bronzed features. "There you are! I knocked on the door and nobody answered."

By now she was crossing the road, eying the huge steers. "What'cha got there?"

When she approached he bent and kissed her lightly. "I brought you a present."

"For me?" She studied the hefty surprise. "Steers?"

"If you're going to be a farmer's wife, it's time to see what it means to raise cattle." His gaze shifted to the cattle, obviously proud of the offering. "I'm sure your ma and pa won't mind. The beef won't be at butchering stage for another few weeks, but they'll make a fine mess of roast and tenderloins this winter."

Flabbergasted, Elly stepped back from the beasts. What did she know about caring for stock or raising beef? The Sullivans kept a few sitting hens for fresh eggs and a milk cow, but beef cattle were so...huge.

One of the steers lifted his tail to deposit a steaming pile of waste. A nasty aroma drifted to Elly, and she caught back a gag.

"Ah, come on, Elly. Raising cattle is what you'll do when we're married." He looked offended by Elly's reaction.

Adele finally made her way down the lane, waddling more than walking. She stood before the white-faced steers, wide-eyed. "My, Gideon, these are fine-looking animals."

"Best of the herd." He looked at Elly. "Nothing's too fine for my girl."

"Well...I..." Where would she put two steers? Elly doubted the pasture near the back of the house would support two animals. The fence was old, grass nonexistent. The real problem was the timing. The cranberries occupied everyone's time. In spite of that, she couldn't bear the disappointment on Gideon's face if she refused the gift. The thought was most generous and considerate. She finally managed to say through tight lips, "Thank you."

Gideon grinned at her expectantly. "Where do you want them?"

Preferably on a platter with potatoes and string beans.

"Put them in the pasture behind the house for now." She had no idea what Pa would say when he saw the "gift."

Gideon slapped the rump of one of the steers and shooed him with his hat toward the back of the house. The other steer lumbered behind. Elly trailed Adele to the cattle's temporary home. "Isn't this wonderful?" Adele whispered. "What a generous man, Elly. He's crazy about you."

If 1600 pounds of meat, bone, and hooves was the measure of a man's love, Gideon idolized her. She hoped she could return that measure of love.

With the cattle safely behind the fence, Gideon closed the gate and draped his arm around Elly when they walked back to the farmhand who held two horses' reins. "I'll see you Sunday afternoon?" Saturdays had been their usual nights to court, but social activities came to a halt with the harvest. Sunday dinner and a long walk afterward served as courting time from late September to the end of October.

The couple paused beside Gideon's horse, and his gaze turned soft and adoring. "Weather's going to turn bad before long. It's hard knowing I won't be seeing you as much in the coming weeks."

"I know. Harvest is always difficult, but the season will pass and we'll be together." She acknowledged the farmhand with a smile.

"Given anymore thought to a date?"

She'd thought of little else. "Gideon..."

"I'm not pushing, just wondering."

"I haven't thought much about a firm date." A blatant lie. *Forgive me.* Their marriage filled her mind before she dropped off to sleep and appeared again when she opened her eyes every morning. "When the berries are on their way to market, I'll turn my full attention to our wedding."

He tipped her chin to meet his tender gaze. "Promise?"

"Promise."

"I'll hold you to that, Miss Sullivan." Mounting his horse, he winked. "Keep those cattle well watered."

Watered? Nodding, she swallowed back panic. The stream was two hundred feet from the pasture and the well even farther. She was still nodding when Gideon whistled and his horse broke into a canter.

Adele's voice interrupted the sudden silence that gathered once the hoofbeats faded. "Well, isn't that just the sweetest thing you've ever seen?"

"I am truly blessed," Elly managed between clenched teeth. "Truly."

She now had two big old steers to feed and water on top of her other duties.

Life couldn't be better.

Chapter 7

Bo studied the building storm clouds in the west and shook his head. Rain was considered a blessing to a farmer unless it came during harvest. Heavy rains meant delay, and possibly damage to the crop. "Hold off the hail, God, and I'd be much obliged."

He glanced up when he heard Elly's voice through the intensifying wind. He whirled to see her plunging through the field, bonnet strings loose, long hair whipping in the wind, racing toward him. The sight of her made his blood race. He tamped down the emotion. Friends. That's all they were now.

She ran like her dress was on fire, calling his name. Catching her up short, he steadied her heaving shoulders. "What's happened?"

"I need help!"

He turned her on her heel, took her hand, and ran with her. "Something wrong with Pa?" he asked, trying to sort in his mind what might cause her to be agitated to the point of seeking his help. Had Pa collapsed? *God, no. Not yet...*

"No! It's my steers."

Bo skidded to a stop. He caught his hat as it was lifted from his head by a gust. "Your what?"

Elly opened pleading hands to him. "My steers are stuck in the middle of the creek. The storm's about to break and I can't get them to budge." She sucked in a deep breath and let it out slowly. "Gideon gave me two steers. I can't let them die of thirst."

"Two steers. That guy knows how to win a woman's heart, doesn't he?" Now that he knew he was rescuing cattle and his pa was all right, he breathed a little easier.

Elly caught up to him, sticking close to his shoulder. "Gideon's working in his far fields. I couldn't find him, and you said that you drove cattle. You know what to do."

The front moved in, and strong gusts whipped the tree tops. When the two reached the creek, she ran upstream. He followed, his heavy boots sinking into the soft riverbank. The weariness of the day's work faded from his limbs. Just past a bend and beyond a clump of bushes, he spotted two steers standing belly-deep in the creek. He didn't care one way or another about the steers, except that Elly cared about their safety. He wouldn't let the escapades of half-witted cattle upset her.

"Get out of the water!" He hoped she didn't see his reluctance to be knee-deep in water in the storm. A man doesn't get hit by light-ning and invite a bolt to him a second time.

"What are you afraid of?" she called. "I need your help. Gideon entrusted these steers to me. I don't want to disappoint him."

"It's lightning!"

Elly shot him a look of disdain and tugged on the rope she'd looped over the neck of one steer. He couldn't abide her poor judg-ment, and he sure didn't intend to take another bolt to the head. The sooner he got involved, the sooner they'd be out of the storm. A flash and then a crack of thunder set him into action.

He approached the stubborn livestock. "Move!" he said to the steer and Elly. He jerked the rope out of her hands. "Get out of the water! You want to be fried?"

"I don't want you fried either. So we better hurry."

A slow, intimate grin broke across his features. "Still as stubborn as a Missouri mule."

"Look who's talking, *preacher*."

He whistled sharp and shrill as he waved his Stetson at the steers. They didn't move, and neither had Elly. "Go to the bank and break off a stout stick. Throw it to me."

"What are you going to do?"

"Whack their behinds, hard." Lightning exploded overhead and pea-sized hail pelted them. In a panic to find the nearest shelter, he grabbed her arm and waded to the opposite side of the bank. "Head for the bluff!" They broke into a run as lightning split the sky, followed by a thunderous clap that jarred the ground. When they reached the shelter of an overhanging ledge, they collapsed, soaked to the core.

Elly straightened, pushing wet tendrils from her eyes. "What are we going to do now?"

Bo folded his arms over his chest in an effort to hide the shakes. "What do you mean *we*? Those aren't my cattle."

Besides, the beef weren't in any real danger. When it suited their purpose, they would plod home. Now, he sat exposed to a colossal electrical storm on the wrong side of the creek with his heart flapping like a screen door in the wind.

"You're being petty," she finally accused.

"When the storm passes, I'll get your cattle out of the stream." He dumped hail from of the brim of his hat and then squinted into the downpour. "If you look closely, you'll see they're already out."

Elly followed his gaze to where the steers lay on the opposite bank, seemingly oblivious to the downpour.

"This is a fine kettle of fish." She squeezed water out of her hair. "There's no end in sight for this storm. How are we going to get back across the creek?"

"It'll rain itself out in an hour or so," he said. "Or not."

"And in the meantime?"

"We sit and wait. The creek will rise. I'm not going out in that lightning."

The rain only intensified. A waterfall curtained the overhang and the wind doused the already drenched inhabitants of the crude shelter. Elly scooted closer to the rock wall of the alcove. She fought a useless battle to suppress a giggle and finally broke into outright laughter. Bo glanced over, eyebrow lifted. "You think this is funny?"

Her hand swept across the view. "I've tried so hard to avoid you, and here your God has thrown us together in a flood rivaling the days of Noah. See how mean He can be?"

"Come now, this little shower can't come close to Noah's flood." He offered her a lopsided grin. "And what's with this 'your God' stuff? He's your God too."

Resting her back on the limestone, she sobered. "Not my God. My God wouldn't get me stuck in a cave with you. Now Richardson's God would have sent fire and brimstone to accompany the hail. And it wouldn't be pea-size—it would be boulders."

He peered outside the ledge. "Reverend Richardson means well, but his approach is unnecessarily harsh. The Good Book says it's His kindness that leads us to repentance. Although we serve the same God, we couldn't be more different in our approaches. I choose to preach joy and resting in the Lord's goodness, where Richardson preaches to scare the devil out of a person in order to get his attention."

Elly was in no mood for a sermon. She had worked in the bogs all day and come home to fight with the cattle for over an hour.

She leaned against the rock. The damp chilled her to the bone, but she was too tired to care. She closed her eyes. "I prefer the softer approach."

"For some, it takes more to get their attention."

Elly listened as Bo struggled to find a comfortable position. "Are you going to sleep?"

"Nothing better to do." He'd been in the bogs all day too. All that grunting and groaning finally led to quiet. Years peeled away and Elly realized they were resting side by side, barely touching, but his presence was so acute, so overpowering, that she squeezed her eyes against the sudden memories that engulfed her. The melodic thrum of the rain soon had her nodding off.

Awakening with a start, she sat bolt straight. Drizzle fell from a darkening sky. Bo stirred beside her, his eyes closed. He murmured, "The storm's let up."

"It's dusk." She scooted to the overhang and took a closer look at the creek. Rushing water roared. The creek was now a river, a roaring body of water.

Crawling out from the overhang, she wiped her muddy hands on her dress. The river was out of its banks. It would be hours before they could cross safely.

Bo soon joined her. Reading her thoughts, he said, "They'll figure the storm stranded us somewhere."

Who was he trying to kid? Faye Garrett still fretted over Bo like he was three years old. "You'll be missed."

"Ma'll figure I'm doing pastoral duties for the Reverend." When she lifted her eyes to meet his, he explained. "Richardson came down with a head cold yesterday. He asked me to cover for him."

"How...nice." She was still unaccustomed to associating Bo with pastoral duties. The good Lord must have seen something spiritual in him that she hadn't years ago.

"Did that taste so bad?" he said.

"What?"

"Saying that I was *nice* to fill in for the pastor?"

"Why should I care? I'm not your boss. You can do what you want."

"Well, Elly girl, I wish that were true."

Rubbing her arms against the chill, she ducked back into the shelter and settled down. They wouldn't be going anywhere for a while.

Eventually he took his place beside her. She was glad for the warmth his nearness brought, but silence separated their thoughts. Finally, Elly said. "What did you mean by that remark? That you're not free to do what you want?"

"Is any man really free to do what he wants?"

"Maybe not all men, but in certain periods of his life a man is free to do as he pleases. I suppose a wife and children, a farm, or an occupation could limit a man's freedom, but you have none of those at the moment."

"No occupation? I'm a pastor."

"So is every religious person I meet. You don't really work. You go around praying over folks. It's not like you harvest a bog of berries every day."

She didn't like the hidden accusations or pure irreverence that seeped through her tone. Being with Bo felt like wearing a comfortable old shoe. Seven years of an ugly past didn't appear to offend her memories. She'd missed his wisdom, his comfort, and his protective arm when the world turned hateful.

Now his affection and protection went to people she didn't know.

The sense of betrayal was as strong as the day he'd ridden back into Berrytop. He belonged to God and anyone who needed his help—but that didn't include her, not unless her steers wandered off.

It seemed Richardson's God thought friendship was enough.

Black nudged the edges of the fading light. Thanks to the steers' contrariness, Elly was cold, damp, and hungry. Spiced cranberry muffins waited for her on the table at home. She'd baked the treats earlier in the day, before she set out for the bogs. They would have tasted good with a cup of coffee after a long day of harvesting.

She could make out the outlines of the two steers on the opposite bank, standing in the drizzle, their heads hung low. *Serves you right.*

She shivered.

"You're cold."

"No colder than you."

"I don't have matches, dry or otherwise, or I could scare up something to eat. There's a farmhouse up the hill. Perhaps they could spare us something." He spoke with such kindness that Elly thought her heart would break. But kindness didn't make up for what Bo had done.

"I'm not hungry." Her stomach growled.

"You will be by morning."

She turned to face him. Seeing him would stop this nonsense going on in her head. "What if the rain doesn't let up? We could be here for a while."

"Could be weeks. Months." She couldn't see his grin, but she could sure hear it.

She turned back to the darkness. "Pray that doesn't happen. I'll reap the benefit if God chooses to answer you."

He could be so unfeeling, such a tease. He'd see. God would flood the ledge. Wash them away. Sear them with a lightning bolt as they helplessly thrashed the water if *she* asked for safety.

Bo lay back and said softly. "God, we need the rain and we're grateful for the shelter. Grant us safe crossing by morning."

She waited for the rant about the place for folks who don't believe in His Word. And that place was hell, where all could expect eternal flames and unanswered cries for help. Reverend Richardson's words raced through her mind. "You get what your sin deserves!"

She glanced over and whispered. "Aren't you going to remind Him where we are?"

"Nothing wrong with His memory. He knows."

"No, but what you said was rather meek, wasn't it? We desperately need help, unless you're fond of sitting in this poor excuse for a cave all night. This is going to be a long ordeal."

"He knows where we are. He heard our request."

"Your request," she corrected.

"Are the two of you not speaking again?"

She wished she could see him better. The growing darkness hid his features. How could she tell if he were being snide or playful? He didn't sound insincere, and after all these years they could still carry on a spirited conversation. Confident. He sounded confident and at complete peace with the delay.

She crossed her arms and thought about the question. Were she and God speaking? "Not a whole lot."

"I thought not. I remember how you'd be on the outs with Him occasionally. Still doing that? He heard the prayer, and when the time is right, He'll answer."

The night completely surrounded them. Nothing but dripping rain and silence filled the alcove. Elly wished he would say something, even if it was snide.

"Has your baking improved any? I'm thinking of a hot apple pie. By the way, those blueberry muffins you brought over the other day were good."

"Pies aren't my best suit. I baked muffins before I left the house this morning. People say they're as good as Ma's."

Of course, people were kind.

"Is Gideon one of those people?"

"Yes. He prefers his muffins bland and on the heavy side." She would convince him to appreciate tastier flaky confections after they married. He'd been eating his own cooking so long he didn't know any better.

"And his meat tough, if I remember right." Elly heard the tease in his voice and bantered back.

"Well done, Bo, is not tough."

"You won't have any problems with suiting his tastes then."

If she could have seen him any better, she would have socked him in the arm. "And what gives you have the right to question my cooking talent?"

"You're right; I have none. A thousand pardons, ma'am. Just making conversation." His boots scuffed against the dirt. He was lying down again. "Watch out for snakes."

Snakes?

She scooted to the farthest corner to avoid any unexpected encounter. Her nap had robbed her of any desire to sleep, but she doubted she could sleep anyway, now that she knew the whole night lay ahead of her.

Her thoughts wandered to Pa, Adele, and the Garretts. Had they noticed both her and Bo were missing? And there was Gideon. She didn't want him to think she was on a secret rendezvous with Bo. He would be crushed.

Bo grunted and shifted. "Sweet dreams."

She halfheartedly returned the sentiment. There was no use spilling her worries and resentments to him. He didn't care. Besides, she had gotten them into this predicament. Her eyes grew leaden and heavy.

His voice drifted to her. "Sure hope we haven't stumbled upon a wolf or bear's den. That would be a real shame."

Her eyes flew open. Was he teasing again or was he trying to rile her?

Either way, she dozed with one eye open and her ears sharp for any and all sounds.

And there were plenty of those.

❦

Sunlight dotted the Sullivans' old kitchen floor when Elly let herself in the back door. Overnight the creek had returned to its banks and crossing became possible. The stove was cold and the house even colder. She noticed the note on the table scrawled in Pa's handwriting.

Might stay in Madison overnight. Not to worry. Don't like to be on the road if it storms.

Relief filled her. Pa had gone to Madison yesterday for extra crates and she'd overlooked the note. Thank goodness there would be no unnecessary explanation of where she'd been all night.

She quickly reached for kindling and lit a fire. Before she left to start a fire in the living room and do chores, she set a pot of coffee on to boil. Finally, she trudged up the stairs to change out of her damp clothes. Her body ached from the sleepless night and she wanted nothing more than a long, hot bath.

That wouldn't happen. She must get to the bogs and see how the berries had fared in the storm.

Two steers?

Gideon Long, what were you thinking?

Chapter 8

Pa had beaten her to the bogs. He and several pickers were bent over a cranberry plant looking for damage when she arrived.

"I thought you were still in Madison."

"I got an early start this morning. Looks like we survived without much damage." Less than a third of the fruit had been harmed by the hail. This was the best possible outcome that could have been hoped for, and the mood among the early pickers was guarded but relieved.

Adele chose her steps carefully across the road this morning, no doubt eager to discover why Elly and Bo had not come home the night before. Elly would have just as soon skipped the subject, but she knew she'd have to say something.

"Morning, Sullivans!"

"Morning, Adele." Holt picked up a rake and Adele waited until Pa moved to another bog before going straight to the heart of the matter. She bent, placing both hands on her knees.

"I came as fast as I could. Bo isn't talking much. You should have been at our house last night. Of course, that would have been impossible because you were stranded on the ledge. Ma paced and fretted. Pa just looked sad. They both thought Bo had up and flown the coop again and taken you with him." She rubbed her round belly and stretched to her full height. "This little one must be getting cramped. I get a foot to the ribs every now and again. I bet it's a boy. No girl would kick like this."

Elly had no idea about babies and kicking. She braced for the question she knew was coming.

Adele leaned in and lowered her voice. "Tell me everything, absolutely *everything*. How in the world did you two allow yourselves to get stuck on the other side of the river?"

Elly shrugged, realizing the story of her night with Bo would be all over town before noon, whether she told or not. Besides, there was nothing to tell.

She told Adele "everything." The steers in the creek. How the storm exploded overhead. And how the next thing she knew, she was under a limestone ledge on the other side of the river. With Bo. She would have said that God had a sense of humor if the incident hadn't involved her.

She fingered the damaged leaves of the plants and plucked bruised berries off the stems.

"That's it?" Adele frowned. "You and Bo spent an entire night together, and there's nothing to add to the story, not one solitary thing? You're holding out on me."

Elly paused and glared at her. "What are you suggesting?"

"I mean...well, didn't the two of you talk about your past and try to set things right?"

Elly studied the sky for chances of another storm, but the morning had dawned clear and crisp with a promise of a glorious Indian summer day to dry out the bogs. She turned toward the house, knowing Adele would waddle behind. She spoke over her shoulder. "We talked about my lack of cooking skills. That's about it."

"That's *crazy*. What couple would waste such an opportunity? Ike and I sure wouldn't have. I can't believe you didn't press Bo to explain himself. That's not like you."

Adele would not let the topic rest, so Elly fed her a scrap. She told her how she and Bo had talked on the swing one night and agreed to be friends. "And nothing more," she finished. "So last night was merely an inconvenience involving two old friends."

Adele made a wry face. "You are such a fibber."

"Am not. I've told everything there is to tell."

"Everything you intend to tell," Adele corrected.

"Are you suggesting that something happened untoward between us?" Elly stiffened. "I am about to be promised to another man, Adele, and besides, you know I would never do anything inappropriate with Bo or any other man. And Bo's a pastor, for heaven's sake." She picked up a rake, lifting her nose in the air, and stalked off.

Adele fell into step. "I didn't mean to imply that you did anything inappropriate. I know you wouldn't *think* of such a thing, but it seems suspicious that you spent several hours alone in an overhang with Bo and didn't mention your former relationship. That's a bit of a stretch even for you." She grunted with each step.

Elly reached back, took her hand, and led her to the house, where they climbed the porch steps and dropped into the chairs Pa had made when he'd courted Ma. "You are my best and dearest friend," she said, "but you aren't privy to every part of my life."

Frowning, Adele leaned back and sighed deeply. "What haven't you told me?"

Adele didn't need to know that last night had been eye-opening. With all Elly's steely determination to make things right between her and Gideon, a secret place of her heart still held out a slim hope that the old Bo would come home.

"I will tell you that last night only reinforced my conviction. Since I know Bo is no longer mine to have, I decided I will shepherd him toward a suitable wife."

"Oh really." Adele cocked her head. "You are so sly. Who might this saintly woman be? I am his sister; I should at least have the right to a sneak peak at my sister-in-law."

"Cecelia. She's beautiful, single, and one of the best examples of a godly woman that I know. She would make Bo the perfect wife. She's been fond of him for years."

"Cecelia? She's been fond of Bo and never said anything?"

"She respected his relationship with me."

"Well." Adele sat back. "You're probably right about Cecelia being a good match, but Bo isn't going to let you choose his mate, Elly. He's a preacher, all right, but his pride wouldn't allow him to do such a thing."

"He's not supposed to have pride."

"But he does—especially when it comes to meddling in his private life."

Elly couldn't argue with her reasoning. Bo retained his pride in a godly way, but fur would fly if he even suspected anyone was planning his future. "Naturally he can't know what I'm doing. One whiff of my plan, and he'll break Cecelia's heart and then come after me with a tongue lashing. That's why I'll need your help."

Adele lifted a dubious brow. "Keep me out of this. Bo doesn't need reasons to be mad at me."

"Cecelia is perfect for him. Far better we tinker a bit and make sure he's happy than leave him to the mercy of the single women here who would fight like gladiators for his attention."

"True." Adele lifted her face to the sun. "But if he'd been interested in Cee, don't you think he would have approached her years ago? You had his heart from the moment he met you."

"That clearly isn't the case now. God now has his heart. Anyone else is going to come second. I'm sure God wouldn't mind a little earthly help to see that Bo is equally yoked. Can you think of another woman in Berrytop who suits him better that Cee?"

Adele leveled her gaze on Elly. "You."

How she wished Adele wouldn't say things like that. All she could do was accept the situation and hope that Adele moved on as she planned to do. "You have to remember, I'm no longer a contender for Bo's heart. Gideon is the only man in my life."

Squealing, Adele clapped her hands. "Then you set the date?"

"No. I would have told you, silly."

"A girl can dream." Adele raised enquiring brows. "And I will still be your matron of honor?"

"You have my word."

"Oh dear, I'll have to wear a tent unless the baby is here by then. I'll be the biggest matron of honor in the history of weddings." Adele's brows furrowed. "I do wish you'd decide on a date. I need to plan ahead these days."

"You'll know the date the very day I set it. I don't care if you have to wear two tents. You're my best friend and I want you by my side."

"Oh my, there's so much to do. How can I help?" Adele patted the pockets of her jacket, probably looking for a piece of paper and a pencil.

Elly reached to still her friend's hands. She didn't want to send Adele into labor over a not-yet-determined wedding date. She spoke with an evenness that belied her rapidly beating heart. "We have plenty of time, but you're right, I will need help." Perhaps Adele could select the gown, confer with the seamstress, decide on the location, the cake...little things Elly couldn't manage with harvest demands. "I'll make a list and we'll go over the details together. Are you sure you feel up to the task?"

Adele hefted herself from the chair. "I desperately need something to do to take my mind off the waiting. And Ike. That's the hard part. Planning a wedding is the best gift you could have given me."

Elly smiled. "I'm sure there'll be plenty to keep us both busy."

Adele stood and walked to the steps, leaning against the railing to go down the stairs. She paused at the bottom and turned back to Elly. "You must tell me the minute you know the date. We have the shower to plan too." She waved over her shoulder. "I'll start work on this right away." As she walked toward the road, Elly heard her muttering, "White cake, of course, with tiny pink flowers. Invitations. The gown..."

Elly called after her. Adele turned, joy lighting her face.

"You have to promise me to keep this quiet. Don't breathe a word to Milt and Faye yet, and certainly not to Bo. I want to have a firm date before everyone gets excited. Do I have your promise?"

Adele made a grand gesture of crossing her heart. "I promise."

Stepping into the house, Elly sighed. She'd just committed herself to marrying off the man she loved to a lovely, desirable woman and marrying herself off to a man who gave her cattle.

The trade didn't seem quite fair.

Chapter 9

Sunday dawned bright, clean, and crisp. Maple leaves blushed to red along their edges. Elly wrapped her shoulders in the shawl Ma had knitted her for Christmas. Her fingers trembled as she pulled the wrap tighter. She sure wished Ma would come home. She had far more wisdom than her daughter about marriage and such. What would she advise about Bo? When she learned the truth about his absence these many long years, the wicked life he'd led, what would she think then?

Knowing Ma, she would easily forgive but like Elly would she ever forget? Both she and Pa made it clear they were eager to be grandparents, but so eager they would accept children from a man who had so easily fallen into sin? Sin didn't have colors. All sin, big or small, was sin, but Bo's former lifestyle should be black. Dungeon black.

Her sins should only be slightly gray. It seemed.

Pa tapped her bedroom door. "Harry'll be ringing the bell here shortly."

"Coming!" Being a moment late to enter their pew was the same as spiritual treason for Pa. She pinned her hat to her hair, picturing the Good Shepherd walking along the Sea of Galilee, pausing to speak to those who gathered. There were no self-appointed times, no anointed places where one could commune with their Savior....

Pa's second sharp knuckle rap brought her back to earth.

The church was a beehive this morning. Elly felt the excitement and heard the buzz of soft voices before she and Pa stepped through the doors. Her gaze landed on Bo sitting in the chair beside the pulpit, right where Reverend Richardson usually sat. Apparently the Reverend was still under the weather.

She considered excusing herself to run home, but that would have been trouble. First from Pa and then just about everyone else—including Gideon, who waved at her from his pew. The sensible choice meant trailing Pa into their pew and sitting down.

News that Bo was preaching must have reached others because the sanctuary was full, unlike most Sunday mornings when there was plenty of room. A long wooden bench sat along each wall to accommodate the overflow. Otherwise it would be standing room only this morning. The good people of Berrytop couldn't wait to hear what the prodigal son had to say.

The singing was more spirited, familiar hymns sung with strong conviction. Elly found herself joining in harmony with Pa's strong tenor. And then Bo stood up.

Bo Garrett's message was simple and incredibly original for this congregation: Love one another.

"Don't simply say that you care; meet your neighbor's need," Bo said. "If your brother or sister in Christ is down and out, cheer him up. If he's hurting, listen and pray. If he's ill, comfort with your presence or help with words if needed. If he's in need, meet that need out of what the Lord has so richly given you."

Elly waited for the real sermon to begin, the one that made her heart beat fast and her palms sweat. This was like sitting at the foot of Christ and being taught. She had never experienced anything like it. The occupants in the room sat spellbound. Not a child fidgeted. No words were whispered. Not a paper crinkled. Everyone was too focused on Bo.

Folks were settling in for another hour, fretting about over-cooked roasts, hungry families, and fussy toddlers when the sermon abruptly ended.

"In closing"—Bo cleared his throat and gave the audience a sheepish grin—"you may not thank me for this, but I feel directed to sing a relatively new hymn."

And then Bo picked up a guitar that had been perched behind the pulpit and sang the sweetest rendition of "It Is Well with My Soul."

In all the years she'd known him, this talent had been hidden from her. The words were sung in golden, reflective tones. She soaked up the pure sweetness the message offered. Ladies sniffed and men reached in their back pockets for hankies to dab their tears. No one added their voices to Bo's.

When he reached the third stanza, his eyes glistened with tears.

> My sin—oh, the bliss of this glorious thought!—
> My sin, not in part but the whole,
> Is nailed to the cross, and I bear it no more,
> Praise the Lord, praise the Lord, O my soul!

As the music strains died away, he dismissed the congregation with a simple, "God, keep us in Your love." For a moment no one moved. The old clock on the wall said they still had another hour to go. Elly didn't want to move. She suspected others felt the same.

Something that defied explanation had just happened within the walls of their church. Just what Elly wasn't sure, but she knew she wanted to sit and soak in the love that Bo had spoken about.

A love that, until this moment, she never knew existed.

The worshippers filed out of the church, pausing to shake Bo's hand. Elly had scooted around the crowd and took her leave by the back door. She wasn't quite ready to face Bo. He was so changed. How had she missed the signs of what God had always intended for him?

Instead, she rejoined the crowd standing in front of the church. What she'd experienced made it even harder to initiate her earlier plan, but dinner was prepared. She spotted Adele, Faye, and Milt and hurried to catch them. "Faye?" she said, a little winded from her rushed exit. "Pa and I would be pleased if your family could join us for dinner."

"Why…that sounds lovely. Let me catch Bo before he accepts an invitation from anyone else." Pride fairly shone in her eyes, and no wonder.

Adele flashed a grin. "How nice of you, Elly. I trust there'll be others joining us?" She winked.

"I made way more chicken and dumplings than Pa and I will ever eat." She swallowed. "I plan to ask Cee to join us."

Adele smirked. "Lovely idea. He'll be there. I'll make sure he is."

Elly glanced around the emptying churchyard. Gideon waved from the steps of the church and started in her direction. "And Gideon. I'm inviting Gideon too." Mercy! She'd almost overlooked him. "He might as well get used to eating my cooking." She faked a laugh.

She spotted her prey coming out of the church with Henry Foster, a young swain who lived a few miles south. Elly waited until proper goodbyes were said and then swooped in to trap her. "Cecelia! I'm glad I caught you. Do you have dinner plans?"

She glanced over her shoulder.

"You can eat with him anytime." Elly hooked her arm through Cecelia's. "You really must join us." She moved Cecelia hurriedly through the crowd.

The young woman looked furtively over her shoulder and spoke with some suspicion. "Where are we going?"

"I invited the Garretts. Bo will be there."

Cecelia's hand covered her heart. "Well," she said matter-of-factly, tucking tendrils of hair back into her bonnet, "of course. I accept your generous invitation."

"Wonderful." Elly drew a deep breath.

Simply peachy.

Milt Garrett pushed back from the dinner table, his plate still full. Elly wondered if she had over-salted the chicken and dumplings. She glanced around the table. The other guests had managed to eat most of their meal. Maybe Milt wasn't partial to dumplings. She would make a note. Surely, this wasn't the last dinner the Garretts would share with her family even though she and Bo were no more.

Holt and Milt wandered into the parlor, where Bo and Gideon had already commandeered the best chairs. Bo had been quiet throughout the meal, saying very little except when someone once again told him how much they had enjoyed the sermon. He seemed embarrassed by his success in the pulpit. Elly thought he better get used to the accolades. People in Berrytop were hungry for a merciful Savior.

"Best I've ever heard," Milt Garrett said, slapping Bo on the back. "Bar none, my boy."

The womenfolk tackled the mound of dishes and chattered while they worked. The main topic was, of course, speculation about Elly's upcoming wedding.

"The plans are coming along beautifully." Adele perched on a low stool at Elly's insistence.

Faye scraped plates. "Are you going to make your gown, honey?"

Elly shook her head. "I haven't given the dress much thought since we haven't set a firm date. Besides, I sew about as well as I cook."

Adele bubbled. "I found an exciting article in the newspaper saying a new shop has opened in Milwaukee. They carry nothing but wedding attire. Imagine that! What do you say, Elly? Shall we send for their catalog? A premade gown is all the rage."

Elly wished Adele would drop all the talk of gowns and bridal attire. To say she hadn't given the idea a thought wasn't exactly true. She'd decided to wear Ma's gown. She could admit to that without the ladies going too crazy on the topic.

Drying a skillet, she wrinkled her nose at the notion of a premade gown. "Ma's gown is more than suitable. When she gets home, we'll do a little nip and tuck here and there but little more. The veil is still in good condition."

Adele's face fell. "Wearing your mother's gown is a symbol of your love for her and so very sweet of you, but a bride deserves her own dress. The article noted that styles are changing." When Elly saw that Adele's audience wasn't moved by her protests, tension released between her shoulder blades.

Faye patted Elly's cheek when she walked by. "I think you're being very wise and sensible, dear. Irene will be thrilled at your choice."

Men's voices rose from the parlor. Faye flashed an apologetic smile. "Oh dear, Holt and Milt are at it earlier than usual. We shouldn't leave them alone." She untied her apron and motioned for the women to follow her. Females gathered at the opposite end of the parlor. They pulled out their stitching, but their real task was to stop a war if one threatened. Milt and Holt didn't see eye to eye on politics, and the presidential election was in full thrust.

Elly was relieved the talk of wedding dresses was behind her. Unfortunately, she knew Adele had sparked a fire. Talk of the upcoming nuptials would be the topic of conversation wherever two or more women gathered.

"Grover Cleveland's a reprobate!" Holt blustered. "The man has the morals of a jackrabbit!"

Milt shook his head in disbelief. "Give him a little respect. By claiming the child as his, he saved that—she's no lady—*woman* from utter disgrace."

Holt wadded tobacco into his pipe bowl, tamping the leaves down with unreasonable force. "Utter nonsense! Cleveland answers his accusers according to the mood of the people. He claims—when it suits him and his ambitions—that he's not certain of the child's parentage. He's only done what any man must. I would like to expect more of my leaders. Let's pray that he remains in New York, a place perfectly suited to an unmarried man with lustful tastes."

"Holt!" Faye snapped. "Insulting the man serves no purpose."

"He'd be an embarrassment in the White House! What's this world coming to?"

Color rose to Milt's cheeks. Faye bit her lip. Her stitching settled into her lap.

"The world will get what's coming to it. The man may eat like a horse, smoke too many cigars, and imbibe a tad too much whisky, but he's the man for president. Cleveland is smart! He'll get this country straightened out."

Faye shot Milt a warning glance, but the others kept their heads down and their fingers busy.

Holt scooted to the edge of his chair. "Straightened out? How do you figure? We're doing better than well under President Arthur. Considering his ill health, he's leaving office more respected than when he entered. Won't be able to say that about Cleveland."

"He could be right, Pa," Bo noted. "Isn't Cleveland the one who says women don't want the vote—or something to that effect? Have to admit he's a brave man to make that statement."

"Arthur stepped right up when Garfield was assassinated," Gideon said. "He's not done badly under tough circumstances. We could have had worse."

Milt frowned. He opened his mouth to respond when Faye cleared her throat. He straightened his vest instead. Elly wished Pa took the hint so easily.

In the lull, Holt chanted, "Ma, Ma, where's my pa?"

"Gone to the White House, ha, ha, ha," Gideon mocked the now familiar phrase, and then immediately sobered.

"Gentlemen—Pa—there are ladies present. This conversation is not suited for gentle constitutions." The way Bo smiled made it clear he wasn't worried about the strength of the women in the room. He disliked the pointless bickering. "Gideon, what's your take on anything but politics?"

Gideon sat up straighter. "I'm just a simple farmer. I don't trouble myself with things I can't control, and that hailstorm a few days back proved without doubt that I don't control much. My wheat isn't in the barn yet." He looked to Elly. "But I'm perfectly happy with the prospect of a wife and young'uns."

Milt waved a dismissive hand toward Gideon and struck a match. "I'm not saying anything the ladies haven't already heard at the mercantile, Bo. Cleveland has probably got himself caught in a messy stew with that Halpin woman, but he's providing that little guy with the support he needs to grow up healthy and educated. In other words, he's doing the right thing. His indiscretion shouldn't disqualify him from being a good leader. If he's good enough for that young upstart, Teddy Roosevelt, he's good enough for me." Milt drew on the pipe stem. "If we disqualified every sinner from running for public office, we would be plum out of politicians."

Bo tilted back in his chair, working hard at stifling a grin. He failed. "I think the Lord might say we should try to weed out the chaff."

Holt slapped his knee. "Milt, you're as stubborn as a rusty nail. You'll be singing a different tune once the election is over. James Blaine will whip Cleveland like a redheaded stepchild when the time arrives."

Milt's eyebrows shot up. "Blaine is as crooked as a shepherd's staff. Why, he's in the railroads' pockets. And talk about immoral! I'd put Blaine right up there with the pack. It'll be Cleveland by a landslide."

Holt shot to his feet. "Hogwash!

"Good Lord, help us! If—and I do mean *if*—that pipsqueak Blaine gets in, it will simply mean the Mugwumps couldn't spot an honest man if they tried."

The men stood toe to toe. Bo and Gideon eased to the front of their chairs. Faye covered her eyes.

Bo got up and stepped between the two men. He faced his pa and put a hand to his shoulder. "You're a strong thinker, Pa, but this is meant to be a social gathering. Elly worked mighty hard to prepare a nice meal for us. We should repay her with pleasant conversation, don't you think?"

Milt shuffled while looking at his shoes. Clearly, he hadn't made his point yet.

Bo smiled broadly and patted the men's backs. "Now, if you two have a mind to provide all this manure for Elly's garden patch, she would welcome the gift. But we're done with politics for the day."

Milt glanced at Faye. "Faye. Get your coat. It's time decent folk were in bed." He stepped around Bo to address Elly. "Sweet girl, those were the best dumplings I ever ate. Don't tell Faye I said so."

"I heard you plain as day, old man. You best get your coat on before I take a broom to your behind." Husband and wife shared a knowing look. Milt looked tired. He needed to rest. Holt Sullivan had pushed him pretty hard.

After Milt and Faye left, Pa took his leave to do some reading. Cee played the piano while the remainder of guests enjoyed her talent. Elly mentally added one more attribute that made Cee an excellent candidate for Bo's wife—she had no strong political leanings. And everyone—Democrat or Republican—could appreciate her musical talent. She insisted Bo sing with her, and his strong baritone floated through the parlor. Elly didn't miss the shared look between Cee and Bo when the clock struck four. She was, however, taken aback by Cee's boldness when she asked him to walk her home. The girl wasn't wasting any time.

"That's a fine idea, Cecelia." He extended his arm. "A good walk with amiable company is just what I need." The couple paused before Elly.

Cee took her hand. "Thank you ever so much for the lovely invitation. I've had a wonderful time, and the meal was delightful."

Elly avoided Bo's direct gaze. She'd seen enough interest in his eye to know he was enjoying himself. Little did he know that his blatant eagerness to walk Cee home fell right in step with her plan. Relationships started this way—even courtships that led to marriages and families.

Bo extended his hand. "Mighty fine meal, Elly."

His eyes finally captured hers. She wasn't sure what she saw there. She finally decided he looked happy. She should join him in his pleasure. The plan was going well. She would even join his blissful state real soon.

"Everyone knows the way to a pastor's heart is through his stomach." She kept her tone light.

Adele followed on Bo's heel, stifling a yawn. "I think I'll go home and catch a short nap."

"Is the baby sleepy?" Elly teased.

"Exhausted, and the child ate far too many dumplings."

Elly watched her friend walk down the path and across the road to the Sullivan farm. An ache rose in her for Adele. Elly's life was unfolding before her, and Bo seemed ready to move on as well. Poor Adele had secured her life with a man she loved, and a senseless wagon accident changed everything.

Elly jumped when Gideon approached from behind to wrap his arms around her waist. "Mighty fine cooking, love."

She leaned into him. "Gideon, you are aware the dinner was appalling. Those dumplings were better suited as bricks than dinner. And the chicken—"

"I wouldn't say appalling. Improving. The dumplings were near done and though dry, I got them down. The chicken was a little chewy but in all, you did a fine job. You can make me chicken and dumplings every night of the week and you'll never hear a complaint."

"That hen was overcooked. I could have shaved erasers in the broth and the texture would have been more pleasing."

He nuzzled her cheek. "Walk with me?"

"I'd love to—but isn't that thunder I hear?"

Another rumble sounded in the distance to prove her point.

Gideon squeezed her tighter. "The storm is still a ways off. Could miss us altogether."

Elly turned toward him and gently lifted his hair off his forehead. He pleaded with his eyes for her to join him. "I'll get one of Pa's slickers."

"I would rather watch the storm from your porch, but my milk cows will be waiting beside the barn. They get downright cantankerous if I'm not on time." He smiled warmly. "It won't be so long before we can watch storms together."

The winds had picked up, but from the road Elly could see that the storm was still building in the distance. Blustery skiffs were coming from the north, but the storm could blow over. Elly draped a light shawl around her shoulders and carried the folded slicker under her arm.

With her skirt and petticoat billowing, Elly let her thoughts inventory the day. Bo's sermon touched her in a new, exciting way. Another one like that, and he would have her fully believing in a merciful God.

Her neighbors and friends shared a not-so-wonderful dinner she cooked, and no one died.

Third, Pa and Milt hadn't killed one another, but she learned something about Washington politics. She hoped she never had to go there.

Fourth, Bo walked Cee home. True, her feelings tumbled a bit over seeing the two of them enjoying each other's company, but no one could claim the couple was not ideally suited.

And lastly, she was walking Gideon home—at least halfway or until the skies opened up.

Life was finally falling in place.

Gone were the hours she'd stood in front of the window and watched for Bo to come home. She no longer spent days hoping a letter would come to explain why he had been away so long. Dashed were the dreams of his homecoming—the embraces, the kisses, his husky voice whispering low in her ear—*Elly*...

"Wouldn't you say?" Gideon's voice yanked her back to the present.

"Sorry...Could you repeat that?"

"I said, I guess you've realized you missed a bullet."

Shaking her head, she tried to make sense of his words. Had someone shot at her? Her gaze skimmed the countryside. There wasn't a soul in sight. "Sorry, I'm muddleheaded. I've been up since before dawn preparing the meal. What's that about a bullet?"

"I said..." He paused. "What are you daydreaming about?"

"Besides my bed? Only how lovely the whole day has been. There's nothing sweeter than good company and unseasonably warm weather—until now. The wind has a bite to it." She unfolded the slicker and slipped into the garment.

Gideon accepted the response. She would have to be more careful in the future, stay in the present, and let the past be the past.

They strolled by a stripped bog that should have been void of berries. She eyed the forgotten row. "I thought Pa and the farmhands picked this fen yesterday. I'll have to finish up in the morning."

Gideon's attention focused on the road. When he looked up, the full power of his brown eyes made her heart thump. "I was referring to the conversation after dinner. If you'd married Bo you would have to deal with a father and father-in-law in direct contention over politics."

"Yes, I've thought about it." Especially this afternoon, when she was tempted to dash a bucket of cold water on the two contenders. They were getting worse as the years passed. Apparently, Pa didn't prescribe to the belief that politics and religion mixed like kerosene and a match. Both subjects were best avoided in social settings.

Voting was a serious matter and should be exercised with careful consideration, but minds often varied. And they varied loudly.

But she had dealt with Milt and Holt's bickering over the years. She and Bo used to escape the brawls by retreating to the swing...where they'd rather have been anyway.

"You agree you dodged a bullet?"

He was still insecure. "Agreed," she said for him. "And if Susan B. Anthony has her day, women will win the right to vote regardless of who wins the election." Only the good Lord knew how hard those women and others like them worked to achieve the goal.

Gideon stopped in his tracks. "What did you say?"

"I said, someday women will have the right to vote."

"Elly Sullivan. I've never heard you talk like that. Why would women need to vote? Their husbands can take care of them."

A raindrop hit Elly in the forehead. "Why? Because..." She bit her tongue. Gideon had proven in the parlor that he didn't like conflict. As his wife she would need to tame her tongue on women's issues.

She opened her palms to feel the first drops of rain. "Drat. I need to start back."

Gideon pulled her close for a kiss and then gently tucked her slicker closer around her neck. "You don't ever have to worry about 'women's rights.' I'll take care of you, provide everything that you need. Your job will be to take care of me and our children."

"Thank you, Gideon. You're very kind." An active household and dirty diapers. What woman could need more?

A light rain pocked the dirt road and pattered on dry leaves as she walked toward home. She should have invited Gideon to stop by later that week. She could make time for it somewhere in her busy schedule.

Odd that the thought had never crossed her mind.

Chapter 10

By the time home came into view, darkness settled like a weary child over the saturated ground. A fine mist chilled the air to the point of misery. Although the glow of lamplight drew her inside, she headed for the shed to stow her wet slicker, a habit engrained in her by Pa. Instead, she followed a distracting, pungent odor around the corner of the barn. Her heart nearly stopped when she saw a mountainous pile of manure heaped in her garden patch—enormous and fragrant. She mentally groaned.

Gideon. Who else? She didn't know another person who possessed that much manure, and he'd wasted no time in getting a load to her. He'd taken Bo's invitation to provide manure for her vegetable garden literally, sent a message by the neighbor child to his hired hand while the other dinner guests visited, and instructed the help to bring the smelly load while she was walking Gideon home.

For heaven's sake! His love was going to kill her. Tears smarted and her eyes burned. What was she supposed to do with all those cow droppings?

A familiar baritone broke into her thoughts. "You're planting a little early this year."

She whirled to see Bo striding toward her carrying two rakes and a shovel. Mist covered the shoulders of his jacket. He must have walked Cee home and returned to his house promptly. Like anyone who raised cranberries, he couldn't resist another look at the stripped bogs.

"Look at this." She swept her hand over the sight. "I know he means well…"

"Gideon?"

She sighed.

"Right thoughtful man. Beef and manure. The man sure knows the path to a woman's heart. I'd probably have gone more with flowers or perfume."

"You're not funny."

He nodded toward the rake in his hand. "I thought you could use some help. Ma's got a weak stomach, and the wind's carrying the stench toward the house. No one will get a bit of rest at the Garrett house until the odor's tamped down."

"This is Sunday, a day of rest." Harvest six days; rest on Sunday. God said so.

He studied the heaped pile. "It's a single load. We can do this in no time."

Her back ached. She needed liniment and a hot cloth.

He handed her a rake. "Saddle up, partner."

With a grunt, she grabbed the hoe and dragged her aching feet to the putrid pile.

"Count your blessings," he called over his shoulder. "It's not steaming."

Manure hardly seemed a blessing at this hour, but her spring garden *would* appreciate the boost. She reached the garden and began spreading the manure over her plot. She eventually stopped gagging and, with grim determination, set to work.

Their rakes pulled and pushed to spread the manure in a thick layer over the garden site. Bit by bit the pile diminished. Bo broke into song, singing an old gospel hymn, "Lord, I'm Coming Home." Elly joined in, hitting the high notes and harmonizing. They used to sing together as kids. They didn't sound bad together then, but Bo had decidedly improved.

So absorbed were they in their musical talent that they missed the arrival of Milt and Faye. Faye pressed a hanky to her nose and mouth. Elly explained how she'd come to be in possession of a mountain of manure.

Milt sniffed. "Lord Almighty, Gideon's lost his mind. You've got your work cut out for you. Need some help?"

Bo and Elly answered in unison, "No!"

"You've had a full day, Pa. We'll be done soon."

Milt cast a doubtful look toward the pile. "I'll leave you two crazy people to it, then. But you might want to quiet down. You'll wake up the whole county." He winked at Bo after he said the last bit.

Milt and Faye walked home, but it wasn't long before other neighbors happened by, and they brought their shovels and rakes to help. Mr. Stack had sniffed the air and heard the singing. Somehow, he'd recognized a need. He carried a shovel with him. "Can you use an extra hand?"

Elly nearly cried. "Oh, Mr. Stack. Yes, thank you."

Allen Bachmeir arrived next. He could still cut a load of wood with one arm, so he said manure wasn't going to faze him and Ma had the kids. Even Pa came out, pulling on a coat to assist. "I must be getting old. I fell asleep in the chair. I never heard or smelled a thing. I smell something now."

Word spread, and before Elly could protest, neighbors were joining her and Bo. Women either brought sandwiches and hot coffee or cheerfully carried a rake and dug in. A manure pile had turned into a town social—one sorely needed at the end of a long picking season.

When full night settled in, lanterns were lit. Faye and Milt returned with hot cocoa and warm cinnamon muffins. Everyone stopped, washed their hands in the watering trough, and enjoyed the treats. Elly noted the weary lines around Milt's eyes. He should have gone to bed hours earlier. He managed to loop his arm around her neck and pretend to give her a knuckle burn. His heart was failing, but he still had a young man's feistiness.

By midnight, the odorous task was finished. The vegetable garden would produce nicely in the coming summer, especially with the whole winter to percolate. Men and women picked up shovels and rakes and headed for home and a short night of rest.

Elly lay flat on her back beside Bo on the side porch, watching the lanterns bob their way down the road and go out—plink, plink—like tiny fireflies settling in for the night. Friends and neighbors wouldn't get much sleep, but their hearts would be filled with the knowledge of fulfilling the commandment to "love thy neighbor."

Leaning back on his elbows, Bo studied the stars. "I'd forgotten how good folks are here."

"I think your sermon this morning might have lit a fire underneath them."

"Ah, you're just being nice, Miss Elly."

"No, really, I hated to see your first sermon end."

"My first sermon in Berrytop."

"I stand corrected."

"You may be hearing more of me than you'd like. Richardson's cold doesn't seem to be improving."

"That wouldn't be so bad. I pray the Reverend improves, but I'm not anxious for him to be back—not anytime soon. I wish you'd been around when I was growing up."

He turned to face her. "I was," he reminded her softly.

"You weren't this Bo." The first honest thing she'd said to him in weeks.

It was too dark to see his face, but Elly heard the melancholy in his tone. "Well, that means a lot to me, Elly. I hope to preach the gospel and see folks receive the Word with new hope."

If love cured the world's problems, then his message should be preached and shouted more often. "Is that how you speak to your flock?"

"That's it. I'm not fancy with words. I repeat what the Bible says. They get it or they don't. I have a young flock that's been through some rough times. They've faced every heartache and betrayal one can imagine. They don't yet understand they have a loving Father who will never leave them or forsake them, but right now they're struggling to gain that knowledge."

Elly knew all about feeling alone with troubles. "God should have left us with more explicit instructions."

Bo's voice smiled at her through the darkness. "He did. He called it faith."

"Faith." She made a dismissive noise. "You once assumed I believed in God. Well, sometimes I do, but other times I can't understand His ways."

Bo chuckled. "His thoughts are higher than our thoughts. You're trying too hard. He left us with the instruction to have faith. He didn't mention a thing about questions."

She got up and shook dried manure off her britches. "You make faith sound easy. That hasn't been my experience."

He sat up and reached for his hat. "I make faith sound easy? Well, it's not. Faith in the face of all that's contrary is nearly impossible. You have to hold on to one word, Elly."

"Faith?"

"Forgiveness. Freedom comes from forgiving and, more importantly, forgiving ourselves. Second chances are a gift from the Father."

Elly cleaned the manure from her body and dropped into bed, groaning. Every muscle throbbed. She thought about getting Ma's liniment and rubbing down, but she was too tired to make a fuss. Sleep would mask the pain.

But sleep didn't come. She tossed and turned, fluffing and then battering her pillow. She finally surrendered to her sleepless state. She puffed a curl out of her face and belatedly realized what robbed her of rest: guilt. She'd promised herself to Gideon and she had just experienced her best, most enjoyable night in seven years, spreading manure with Bo.

Wasn't this a fine mess? The work she'd put into forgetting flew right out the window.

Gideon was a good man. He'd demonstrated an odd sense of romance and generosity, but she refused to back out on him a second time or cause him any heartache. Bo would always have her heart, but she had learned to live with the fact. She could learn a new life—a new way. And if God were truly merciful and kind, He'd help her change into a fine young woman who loved Gideon Long with all of her heart and soul.

A man—or a woman—was only as good as his word. Pa and Bo had taught her that much.

Chapter 11

Two hours of sleep made for a very early morning. Elly rose before the rooster to bake Gideon a cranberry-raisin pie, a small compensation for having had a good time without him. She should have sent word about the work party his pile of manure had caused. He would have come. She just plain forgot to do so. Her forgetfulness said nothing of her feelings for him. Of course she loved Gideon. How could she not? He'd more than proved his love with his patience, the two steers, and now all that manure.

The new day brought a fresh perspective. The manure, though worrisome at the time, was his way of saying "I love you." The same explained the cattle. There were easier, less backbreaking ways to express a man's devotion, but she couldn't fault him. She would reward him for his thoughtfulness with a fresh-baked pie.

Yawning, she poured another cup of hot coffee and stirred the bubbling pot of cranberries and raisins, adding a pinch of salt and a little flour for thickening. Still half asleep, she rolled out the crust, dumped in the bubbling mixture, and added three dollops of butter. Then she rolled out the second lump of crust, cut crisscross slices, and laid them neatly across the filling. Shoving the pie into the oven, she sat down to add sugar to her coffee.

Pa wandered through on his way out to the bogs. "Aren't you working today? It's Monday, girl. Got a whole week ahead of us."

"I'll be along shortly."

The pie sat on the counter cooling for the rest of the day. Finally, after the sun had sunk low and Elly finished cleaning up after a light supper, she told Pa she was off to deliver the pie to Gideon.

"Get home before dark," he called. "There are night creatures out there."

Night creatures? "How old am I now, Pa?"

"I don't care if you're as old as Methuselah. I don't want you out alone once it gets dark."

"Yes, sir." Still grumbling, she tied her bonnet strings and put her shawl in place. *Methuselah? I bet he didn't have a curfew.*

She left the house and began the tiresome two-mile walk. Gideon was her beau, her intended. He lacked for nothing but love and children. She would be the one to fill those holes. And soon Gideon's life would be complete. Sighing, she glanced at the pie. Very pretty, if she did say so herself.

Setting her jaw, she traipsed on. Eventually she tapped on Gideon's back door. The cool air bit at her cheeks as she waited, lifting the towel to eye the pie. He would be so surprised.

Astonishment lit his eyes when he answered her knock. He focused on the cloth-covered basket, and his smile broadened. "Whatever is in that basket, I hope it's for me."

"Of course it's for you." She held the dish out for inspection. He lifted the cloth and sniffed. "Cranberry and raisin?"

"Right as usual," she said. "It's a thank-you for the manure."

"Did I surprise you?" His expression said he might burst with pleasure. "There's plenty more where that came from." She trailed him inside to the warm kitchen.

Elly considered telling him about the spontaneous party the manure created, and how, if Bo hadn't have helped, she would still be spreading. But she didn't. She doubted Gideon would appreciate the irony. Instead, she poured coffee while Gideon gathered plates and forks. Her gaze took inventory of the kitchen. He kept the place surprisingly neat, but there were no lingering fragrances of cooking meat, no evidence of pots drying on the counter.

Gideon served her a small piece and lifted half of the pie onto his plate. She took the first bite. Her jaws locked, her eyes watered. She puckered. He discreetly set his fork aside.

She sighed. "I forgot to add sugar."

"Well, no matter! I like my pies tart." He picked the fork back up and stuffed a bite into his mouth. Water filled his eyes as he chewed. "Good. That crust is nice and flakey. Never eaten better."

She was too tired to stop him. She propped her cheek in her hand and watched him force down the entire piece of bitterly sour pie. The man was hopelessly smitten. Lifting a hand, he sucked in a deep breath. "Can you get me a dipper of water?"

It was the least she could do.

He tilted his chair back and patted his stomach. "Mighty fine fixin's, Elly. Your cooking's gettin' better every day."

She snatched up the remaining pie, stepped out the back door, and walked to the pig trough, where she tossed the contents. After one bite the animals squealed and scattered like chaff. It was a sad day in Wisconsin when the pigs wouldn't eat her cooking.

Following her outside, Gideon drew her into his arms. "You got awful close that time, sweetheart. I wouldn't let anything like a sour pie dishearten me. The crust was perfect, and from what my mother says, that's the hard part. You'll be a fine cook in no time at all."

The solemn hope in his voice made her laugh. He was such a kind soul—tolerant, funny, and so in love with her. She could, and she would, return the love he deserved.

"Gideon..." She reached for his hand. "Walk me down the road a piece. I promised Pa I'd be home by dark."

"You've had a long day. I wouldn't hear of you walking. I'll hitch the buggy and drive you home."

Trailing him to the barn, she waited while he gathered tack and let the horse out of the stall.

"I've been thinking," she ventured. "I'd like to be married at home." She couldn't bear the thought of Reverend Richardson officiating at her marriage. And if Bo offered to step in...well, that was a whole new problem. She wanted to focus completely on Gideon that day. No distractions.

He slipped the bridle bit into the horse's mouth. "I don't know, Elly. It seems to me the church is the best place two people could hope to bless their marriage. And I wouldn't want anyone to feel left out. Your parlor isn't that large."

She chose her words carefully. "We don't need a big show. We're older. We know what's important to start a marriage. I picture our families gathered around in my parents' parlor. Perhaps we can meet later at the church for cake and punch with our friends."

Gideon fretted with the horse's mane. "Still...the church...I never thought of another setting."

"Couples choose their site, Gideon. Church is always nice, but there's something very sweet about taking vows in the home."

Turning to face her, he smiled. "I would marry you in an igloo, Elly Sullivan." He drew her into a long kiss. His touch warmed her stomach, but the butterflies were asleep. When he gazed into her eyes, she saw a deep and solemn love. She had made the right choice in Gideon Long.

Elly settled beside Gideon on the wagon bench and he stuffed a warm blanket over her lap. "There. Are you warm enough?"

"Very. Thank you."

Soon after, the gelding trotted off and she huddled close to him for better warmth. He pulled her closer with an arm around her waist. She hadn't expected a romantic ride through the darkening landscape, especially after such a dreary day of work in the bogs. The evening star winked brightly. She closed her eyes to rest her head against his shoulder. The material of his coat was scratchy. Bo's was soft and...She caught her thoughts.

"Pesky geese!" Gideon nudged the horse to a trot.

She sat up to see a gaggle of Canada geese huddled in a tight group on the road. They fed on grain dropped by wagons headed to market. The geese honked, stretching their necks toward the sound of the approaching horse and wagon.

"Watch this," he said.

"Gideon, don't you dare." Too late, Elly remembered his annoying boyhood pranks. He fully intended to drive right through those birds, scattering them into a frenzied flight.

Grinning now, his arm left her shoulders and he gripped both reins tightly. An almost maniacal smile stretched across his features.

Elly scooted to her side and gripped the wagon bench. "Do not charge those geese!"

Gideon ignored her. The horse surged ahead and plowed into the gaggle. Honks and fluttering wings filled the evening air. His uproarious laughter froze her heart. Covering her eyes, she held her breath as feathers flew. The buggy shot through the chaotic flight and honking calls of distress.

She felt a distinct plop on the top of her bonnet and groaned.

She didn't want to think of what had just occurred. She kept her gaze straight ahead until the wagon shot clear of the disturbance.

Gideon pulled up on the reins, saying, "Whoa there, Clarence." The horse gradually slowed and her fiancé bent double, laughing.

She failed to see one humorous thing about the incident. The appalling episode must have shaved years off the geese's lives. Scowling, she took off her bonnet for inspection. A green plop of goose dropping sat on the crown. Her bonnet had seen better days, but today was an insult. Gideon's fit of hilarity turned to concern. "Oh, did one of the geese get you?"

She managed a weak smile but no amusement. "I believe this was meant for you."

He hauled on the reins, brought the wagon to a full stop, and set the brake. Once he tied the reins in place, he brought out a hanky to scrub at the stain. "Sorry, I couldn't resist."

"Yes, I saw that you were torn." She yanked the hanky away, dampened a corner with her tongue, and tried to remove the ick. Her efforts spread the spot. The damage was worse than she'd thought.

"Honest Elly, if I'd thought you'd have gotten—"

"Take me home, Gideon." She returned his wadded-up hanky.

He cast a repentant eye in her direction. "I really am sorry—just having a little fun."

Fun? Charging peaceful wildlife and being the target of a frightened animal's droppings had not been enjoyable. This was no time, not when she was angry, to clarify how she liked to have fun. She couldn't stop her thoughts returning to the previous evening. Warmhearted neighbors, the support of friends, a surprise treat—that was her type of fun.

"I'm fine. Don't worry about it," she said, knowing she hadn't convinced him she was fine or that he shouldn't worry.

The rest of the trip was made in silence. Tiny specks of snow now flew through the air. The buggy pulled up to the house, and she leaned over and gave him a peck on the cheek. "Thank you for the ride home."

"I really am sorry. I should have been more thoughtful."

"I'm really tired, Gideon. Only a few days of harvest remain. We'll discuss this when we're rested."

Chapter 12

The push to complete the harvest before bad weather set in focused everyone's attention. Round, plump cranberries heaped in rows of crates sat along the bogs, evidence of another God-given harvest of exceptional abundance. Pickers worked from early morning to last light to finish.

Others, older women mostly, washed and hand-sorted the berries before they went into crates. All dutifully bent over their work and returned home late afternoon to care for families. The wind had shifted and now blew in icy puffs from the north. Heavy coats and long johns replaced britches and wool shirts. Winter's fury knocked on the door.

Elly straightened mid-morning, holding her aching back. It would take until Christmas to work the kinks out of her muscles. She spotted Milt Garrett alone in his bog, bending over a plant. She watched as he slowly sank to the ground, holding his head. Pitching her gloves aside, she raced across the road, her heart pounding. *Please God, don't let this be the day.*

Skidding to her knees, she bent over Bo's father. Her heart slammed her ribs. *Please God, not now.* "What is it, Milt?"

Shaking his head, he wheezed. "Just catching my breath."

"Here." She reached through his open coat to loosen his collar and then ran to the bucket and drew a large dipper. Bringing the refreshment to his mouth, she whispered, "There now. That's better."

He drank sparingly, pausing to catch his breath before taking another sip. She remembered Bo's earlier caution: *Pa doesn't want anyone to know how sick he is.* When she offered him another drink, he pushed the dipper aside.

"The days are getting colder," she soothed. "Sometimes it's hard for me to breathe. There now. One more tiny sip?"

He brushed the offer aside. Resting on his haunches, he sucked in shallow breaths until his shoulders relaxed and his breathing eased. They sat in silence, Elly watching his every move. He eased to the bog floor. He didn't seem to be in any hurry to move on. He looked up to meet her gaze. "Thank you, darlin'."

She sat beside him. There were still berries needing to be picked, but they could wait.

Gazing across the bogs, Milt said softly, "I always thought you and Bo would be raising these berries together someday."

"Yes." She loosened her bonnet strings and pulled off the hat. She'd scrubbed hard at the spot the goose dropping left, but unfortunately the bird possessed a robust liking for purple berries. This would be her working bonnet from now on. "I thought the same. Guess someone more powerful thought otherwise."

Milt shook his head. "I don't know what got into my boy."

"The good Lord got into him," she said. "After a bit."

"It's that 'bit' that concerns me. Following his natural man cost him just about everything he held dear."

"He still has his family. He loves you all very much."

Drawing a shallow breath, Milt nodded. "I should be thankful the Lord snatched him back."

"Well, He says His sheep know His name."

Milt's eyes skimmed the fields. "He's a good boy, Elly. From the moment I heard his first cries, I knew he was going to be different. God was going to use him to make the world a better place. That young'un was born with a purpose."

Elly could only agree. "I've never heard finer messages on Sunday mornings. No yelling. No hollering. Just the simple truth offered in love."

Silence lengthened between the two as they sat looking over the bogs. Cranberries were Elly's life, and it had been a good life. Soon she would be raising cattle, which she knew absolutely nothing about except they had a mind of their own. Come January, she would learn. She doubted she could give up berries completely. Ma and Pa would need her in the bogs as long as they owned the farm. How would Gideon feel about his wife splitting time between cattle and berries? She guessed she ought to ask. He might think twice about her as a life's partner.

Milt took another deep breath and slowly got to his feet. Elly rose to help him, but thought better of doing so. Men valued their pride, sick ones more than most. "Don't know how I got on the subject, but I—me and Faye want you to know that our hopes were dashed just as yours were. We had already begun to think of you as our daughter."

"Thank you, Milt. I felt the same." But Gideon was her future, not Bo. "I still love you and Faye. Nothing Bo could have done would ever change that."

"Don't get me wrong." Milt shook his head. "We're fond of Gideon. He's a good man. He'll make a fine husband and father."

"Thank you." Adjusting her britches, she smiled. "I'll always be here for you and Faye. I hope you know that. I'll just be down the road a piece."

His eyes softened. "You're good clean through, Elly. You'll always be our girl. Always. Nothing's going to change our love for you."

But so much would change. The cattle farm would possess her. The cows would need milking twice a day, no matter what the season or circumstances. There was the garden, larger by half, to tend. And chickens. That would all fall to Elly, as well as cooking three meals a day. Of course, children meant her attention would be focused on their needs. And her loyalty would belong to Gideon with no reservations. Milt might find comfort believing nothing would change, but Elly knew better.

She turned her softest gaze on his gray face. "Nothing will change between you and me."

"You're a wise one, missy. Folks get uppity when life doesn't flow along as they think it should. We all want to believe we're paddling the boat. We don't like surprises when it comes to our plans. Sometimes, though, God lets us see how His ways are better."

"Milt, do you think we'll get to ask God questions when we see Him face-to-face?"

He rubbed the day's growth of beard. "I don't plan asking Him a thing. I'm gonna thank Him, and then I'll raise fine cranberries on this new earth, the finest anyone's ever tasted."

Squeezing her shoulder, he set his hat to a dapper angle and walked off. He wasn't an old man, but he walked with his head bent, feet shuffling to stir up dust, and his shoulders braced against the north wind.

Elly dawdled for a moment longer, gazing out over the bogs. Soon the site would wither and turn brown and lifeless. She didn't want her life to imitate the berries—living from season to season, withering with age, and lying dormant with the harsh seasons. She would not live in fear of frost or worry about fruit worms. She would love Gideon and the children they had and tend their home—even if that meant burning three meals a day—and be grateful.

She could do something that simple.

Bo was down on his hands and knees in the bog when Cecelia came into view. His eyes landed on the steaming dish she carried between two cloths, and unless he missed his guess the contents were another casserole—the third this week. The woman was clearly husband hunting.

He had to admit that Cee was appealing to a man's eye, but he wasn't in the market for a wife. Not just any wife.

Rising, he prepared to defend his stomach. She was an excellent cook, but Ma was getting a little testy that her kitchen was being overtaken by a pretty young woman with matrimony on the mind.

Cecelia's grin widened when she spotted him, and her steps picked up. "There you are!"

"Morning, Cecelia." He glanced at the sky. "Or guess it's closer to noon."

She extended the dish, proud as a peacock. "Roast and vegetables."

"Cee, you don't need to bring my lunch. Ma..."

"Nonsense. I adore cooking and it's my pleasure to bring your meals occasionally."

Occasionally it would be a pleasure to down her offerings, but not in a bog.

Her gaze roamed the area. "Where can we sit?" Apparently she had every intention of joining him.

"There's no shade here. Why don't we go to the house and have Ma and Pa join us?" That would go over with Ma like a square-dancing squirrel. During picking season socializing ceased, but he couldn't be impolite. He'd eat the beef and vegetables and send her on her way.

"There's a perfect place right over there." Cee focused on an area just outside the bog and nowhere near the Garrett home.

The two settled on a grassy knoll. Cee whipped out a white cloth and laid it out. Meat, vegetables, bread. Cheese and a raisin pie followed. He eyed the heavy fare and knew he wouldn't be doing much work this afternoon with the picnic resting heavy in his stomach. She dipped up a two-man portion and handed the plate to him. "Looks good, Cee."

"When you finish, there's pie and cold milk." A canning jar rested in the basket. "I iced the milk overnight in the stream, so it should be extra cold."

Taking a bite, he nodded. "Real thoughtful of you. Thanks." He nodded toward the plate as he chewed. "Tasty."

"Thank you. There's plenty more where that came from."

"Aren't you going to eat?" She seemed more interested in his nourishment than hers.

"No, thank you. I'll just keep you company." Sighing, she drew her legs to her chest and stared at him.

The scrutiny made him uneasy. He shoveled food into his mouth, chewing. Then another bite. And another. "Isn't that a fox near the second bog?"

Whirling, her gaze sought the sight. "I don't see it."

"Huh. Must have been a dog." He polished off the feast and handed her the clean plate. "Wonderful meal, but I have to get back to work."

"Wait! You've eaten one tiny plate and there's still milk and pie."

She reached for the pie and he stopped her. "Any way you could wrap that up and send it home with me?"

Her hurt expression touched him. She was a fine woman, and he'd never tasted better food. A man would be proud to have her attention, but he couldn't let her raise expectations that he couldn't meet. "Cee. Can we speak frankly?'

"Of course, Bo." She turned an earnest expression on him. "Was the meat tough?"

"No, the meal was perfect. You're perfect, but I have the feeling you might think…" How did you squelch a woman's expectations without hurting her feelings?

"I might think what?"

"That I plan to settle down real soon." He reached for her hand and held it. "You're a lovely creature. Your eyes are the prettiest green, and your smile would melt any man's heart. But I'm not the man you need, Cee."

Color bloomed on her cheeks. "I'm that obvious, huh?"

"Not obvious. Sincere. And I don't want to waste your time. It's going to be a long while, according to my schedule, before I think about marrying and settling down. Might be, I won't ever. The ministry keeps me busy, and now the bogs."

Sighing, she began to pack up. He noticed the pie went back into the hamper. "You must think me a fool."

"I think I'm one lucky man to have all this fussing over me." He patted his burgeoning middle. "I'm going to outweigh ole Gerty if I keep this up." Ole Gerty stood near the Garrett barn, chewing her cud.

Cee smiled. "Well, thank you for the honesty. Most single men around here would have eaten the pie and milk before they told me they weren't interested."

Grinning, he reached out and tweaked her nose. "Honestly, I was about to change my mind and ask for that pie." He flashed a grin. "I'm a fool for raisins."

Chapter 13

Elly nearly dropped the skillet she was washing when the kitchen door burst open late that evening. Adele and Cee rushed in. Behind them leaves flew and trees bent in the wind's fury. Adele's cheeks glowed with health, her belly now starting to resemble a ripe watermelon. She wildly embraced Elly. "You did it!"

"Did what?"

"Set the date! You actually set the wedding date with Gideon!" Squealing, the two women encircled Elly.

"Hold on!" She pushed back the assault. "Where did you hear such a rumor?"

"It's all over, silly. You took Gideon a pie, you discussed the wedding, and he drove you home in his wagon."

"Discussed, Adele. We discussed where we might have the ceremony. We haven't set a firm date."

The two guests' expressions fell. Elly shook her head as she added a lump of lard to the hot skillet.

Dropping to the nearest chair, Cee released a whoosh and addressed Adele. "I told you Clell East was an old windbag and didn't know what he was talking about." She looked at Elly. "At least you're doing better than me in the love department. Bo told me in no uncertain terms he wasn't in the market for a wife and I could take my casseroles and pies and fly to the moon."

"He did not." Elly smothered a grin, more pleased than she should be by the announcement.

"Well, close. I got the drift. There was so much food I dropped the leftovers by Gideon's. At least he enjoyed them."

"Everyone is beginning to give up hope, Elly." Adele removed her cloak. "Why are you being so pokey? Marry the man."

Elly stepped to close the door against the blustery wind. "Mind your own casseroles and I'll take care of mine." She returned to the stove and scooped flour into a bowl. "If it makes you feel any better, I am about to set the date."

"Liar, liar pants on fire."

Elly flashed a secretive grin. "When I tell the groom, I'll inform you next."

"Clearly, your memory is slipping. I was supposed to be the first you told when you set the date. Lucky for you, I don't hold grudges." Teething her gloves off, Adele stepped to the cookstove to warm her fingers. "New Year's Eve. That would be perfect for a wedding."

Cee left her chair and held out her hands to be warmed. "Tell me how I can help, Elly. I want to be a part of the festivities."

"Of course. Thank you. I'll let you know." Everything was working out perfectly. Memories of Bo were already fading. Still, in the secret places of her thoughts, she wondered what would have happened if she'd offered him a fresh start when he'd first come back to town. No one on earth was perfect.

She slid the last chicken leg into the skillet and joined Adele at the table. "Want a cup of tea?" she asked Cee, who was still warming herself by the fire.

The lady shook her head. "No, I was on my way to the mercantile when I bumped into Adele. Mother needs some staples. As for me, I had to come over and confirm the rumors were true."

"They're not."

"Confirmed."

"But you're not ruling out a New Year's Eve wedding." Adele was like a dog with a worrisome bone. "You could use your Christmas decorations for the church."

"True, I never take the tree down until after Christmas." Elly played along. "But I'm going to be married right here, in my home, just as Ma and Pa were."

Adele leaned on her hand. She chewed her lip.

Cee backed toward the door, waved, and left in a rush of leaves. Wise woman.

Grinning, Elly knew she needed to assure Adele of her honorable intentions. "We'll have a small reception at the church and then go home." Gideon's home. And she would be Elly Long. Gideon's wife. She couldn't quite reconcile herself to the new identity.

Hadn't she moved on? She and Bo were friends, only friends.

Adele frowned. "Oh my goodness, you're going to back out on him again."

Elly took Adele's face in her hands and slowly formed the words. "I am going to marry Gideon."

"You're not. You're not the least bit excited about the wedding."

Elly pushed back from the table. "What must I do to convince you? I could do cartwheels between here and the parlor."

"The last time you did cartwheels in the kitchen, you broke your mother's favorite bowl. To protect Irene's interests, I command you to behave."

Elly returned to the stove to flip the browning chicken. No sense in tormenting Adele any longer. "You will still be my matron of honor?" Elly turned to take in her friend. She couldn't help but smile at the spectacle she would create as part of the wedding party with her ever-expanding stomach.

Adele's face shone. "You said I could wear two tents."

The women laughed. "Make sure you add lace. And a few pearls. I'm wearing Mother's dress," Elly said.

"No catalogue?"

Elly arranged the fried chicken on a platter. "Mother's dress is pretty and will do nicely."

A tap sounded at the back door as Elly plunged her hands into biscuit batter. She glanced toward Adele. "Can you get that?"

Adele hefted herself off the chair to open the door. There stood her father, Milt, bent but smiling.

He stepped inside and brought a rush of wind with him. Elly groaned inwardly. She'd swept leaves all day. What would follow? The winds foretold a storm to come. Ice skimmed the watering trough, harkening the coming of winter.

Milt looked to Elly, his hat in hand. "I didn't mean to disturb your cooking. I put Holt's shovel in the shed. I thought he should know." Milt rocked back and forth on his feet like a boy anticipating Christmas. Something was up. The presidential election had taken place recently, but this was too early for results. Rumor was the count tallied so close that the win could go to either party.

Adele shook her head. "Papa, you promised Ma you'd be neighborly."

Elly led Milt to the parlor, where Pa was enjoying a late afternoon nap. She woke him to announce Milt and then backed out of the room and closed the doors. After the requisite niceties, fur would fly. She could only hope that blood wouldn't flow.

Adele leaned against the wall. "I'm so sorry."

"The election can't be decided yet."

"Yes, it is," Adele said, wide-eyed. "Mrs. Standish stopped by half an hour ago with the news. Cleveland won by a slim margin."

Elly knew then why Pa had come home from town looking glum. He'd taken to his chair and fallen asleep there. She listened to the rising voices coming from the parlor. Her eyes widened.

Adele raised an eyebrow. "The news does mean Papa will be intolerable for a while. He'll have every Republican in town avoiding him."

Elly sank into a chair. "You? What about me? I'll have to listen to Pa's laments for weeks." Elly shook her head when male voices intensified from the den.

"There is one bright spot. I heard Mr. Cleveland plans to invite his sister, Rose, to the White House to serve as official hostess. I've seen pictures of her in *Ladies' Magazine* and the *Literary Gazette*. She's lovely. I'm sure she'll liven up the place nicely until Mr. Cleveland finds a Mrs. Cleveland." Adele sent another worried glance toward the doorway. "When do you think the big storm will break?"

"By how many votes?" Pa thundered.

Elly looked to Adele. "Oh, I'd say…about now." She shoved the skillet to the back of the stove. "I doubt Pa will want supper. I have a feeling he's lost his appetite."

By the end of the day, Elly had had her fill of politics. But the people of Berrytop spoke of nothing else. Grover Cleveland had done the impossible. He'd broken the longest losing streak for any major party in American political history by becoming president-elect. Add the fact that he'd accomplished the feat at his young age—forty-four—and the reality that he was single, and people couldn't stop talking. Democrats walked around with monkey-like grins. The world, others predicted, was going to Hades in a handbasket.

Elly relished the peace she found in the bogs. She took the opportunity to walk beside the empty vines, checking for stray rakes and tools. The Sullivans had been blessed with another abundant crop; bills would be met and Pa could turn his attention to the new crop.

Darkness came swiftly in early November. Endless days of cold winds and icy landscapes lay ahead. She stored a rake and closed the shed door. Turning her thoughts toward the upcoming nuptials, she stopped in the middle of the yard. Who would perform the ceremony? Reverend Richardson would be the likely choice, but he posed a problem: she favored anyone but him. There was Bo. She shook the ridiculous notion aside. She would never have Bo marry her off to another man.

She walked on, mulling over the choices, which were few. She turned toward the Garrett farm and saw that someone there, probably Adele, had lit a lamp against the creeping darkness. If not Bo, then why not Milt? The town knew the Garretts and the Sullivans always enjoyed a close relationship. Milt would be the perfect officiant. As far as she knew, no rules governed who could marry a couple. And this would likely be Milt's last year on earth. The thought brought a swift rush of tears to her eyes. What a beautiful way to honor a man who had come so close to being her second father.

Milt. Of course, she would ask Pa first, but he would be too emotional to give his daughter away and perform the ceremony.

No, Milt was a perfect choice.

"Milt? Milt Garrett?" Gideon looked at her as if she had ants nesting in her eyebrows. He'd stopped for a brief visit on his way home from town. The two stood in the parlor, face-to-face. If there had been a chance at having a romantic moment with her intended, testing her idea of having Milt officiate the wedding doused her hopes.

"I know it doesn't sound logical." She wanted to tell him about Milt's weakened heart, but she'd promised Bo that she wouldn't. "You know my feelings about Richardson. The only other pastor in town at the moment is Bo. You don't want Bo to marry us. So Milt is the obvious choice. Our families have been...well, like family since I was very young." She gently pressed her hand to his chest. "Of course, if you know of anyone else—"

"Elly, this is too peculiar. Everybody in Berrytop knows how you and Bo...and Milt is his—"

She stopped him with a raised palm. "Ancient history. I understand your hesitancy, but I'm asking you to trust me when I say this is the best solution to the problem."

"Problem? You're referring to our wedding as a problem?"

Now he was being petulant. "Not at all, but I won't have Richardson."

Gideon studied his work boots. Elly wondered if she hadn't finally pushed him beyond tolerance.

"I would feel the same if you wanted a former lady friend's father to marry us. But Milt is our best choice, Gideon."

He raked his hand through his hair. "This is highly irregular. Will such a ceremony bind us together? Milt isn't a preacher."

"Of course we'll be married." At least, she didn't think the Bible specially said who could marry a couple.

His hands balled into fists at his side. "The idea's just plain crazy, Elly. I'm opposed to Milt Garrett performing our ceremony. And shouldn't Bo be heading back to his congregation? The harvest is over. He said he would leave after the harvest. What's holding him up?"

She hated seeing Gideon so agitated, mostly because she thought he was being ridiculous in his obvious jealousy. She was marrying him, not Bo. "I don't know; I haven't asked. Adele says maybe he's decided to stay through the bad weather."

Adele had told her no such thing, but she needed to cover for the family's real dilemma. The whole community would know the real reason Bo remained, and very soon. Milt was weakening more every day. Keeping his condition quiet was growing nearly impossible. His decline was obvious.

There wasn't a sound reason to start a marriage with this sort of tension. Releasing a pent-up breath, she conceded with a sense of relief. "If that's how you feel, I respect your wishes. The traveling minister will be around next spring. We can marry then."

"Oh, no you don't." His brows lowered. "We're not putting the wedding off another four months. Milt can perform the ceremony." He pecked her cheek and strode toward where his coat hung on a hook. "All that matters to me is to know with certainty that you'll be Mrs. Gideon Long soon."

"Good." She touched his arm. "There are a couple more items to talk about. I've been thinking that maybe New Year's Eve..."

"I've swallowed quite a lot here, Elly. Can this wait?"

"Not really." She motioned toward the parlor. "Let's get comfortable. We don't need to rush."

"I would rather stand. I have cows waiting for me."

Cows. Always the cows. "All right. What do you think about Harry Finnish for your best man?"

"Finnish? The blacksmith? I barely know the man."

"Yes, but he's been attentive to Adele during her mourning. Since she's my matron-of-honor, and since she and Harry are about the same height, they would be perfect. And this would give them time to be together, get more acquainted."

"I had Fred in mind."

"Fred Latiey?"

"Why not? We've been friends since we were kids."

"If that's your wish, but isn't Fred, well, lacking in height? And Adele is tall for a woman."

"What does height have to do with anything?"

"If you're happy to pair a giraffe and a hippo, then naturally you can ask Fred."

"Fred isn't fat!"

"I didn't say he was fat. I was referring to his height. Do you have any problem with Sally Hawkins overseeing the food for the celebration?"

"As long as we're using animals now, let me remind you that she laughs like a hyena."

"Gideon!" Elly snapped. "You're talking about your former Sunday school teacher. Sally has baked nearly every wedding cake in Berrytop since I can remember. What will she think if we don't ask her to bake ours?"

"But that laugh, Elly. It gets to me."

"Do you have a better suggestion?" She was beginning to see that including the groom in any of the decisions for the wedding was a mistake.

"Ma. She can bake the cake. I love her cakes," he said. "As soon as I write her about the date, she'll set out for home."

"Gideon," she said, soothingly, hoping he would recall that his ma's cakes never got cut at church socials.

"Well, she does." He reached for his hat. "What about Cecelia? She bakes some mighty fine cakes and pies. Finest I've ever tasted—beats Sally's by a country mile. "

"I'm asking Cecelia to be my bridesmaid. Bridesmaids shouldn't be responsible for the cake too."

Defeat clouded his eyes. "It seems you've gotten your way. Just tell Sally to keep her hilarity down."

"Thank you. You won't regret having Sally bake the cake and be the server. Your mother and Cecelia should be free to enjoy the wedding, not fuss over details."

When he closed the door behind him the window glass rattled.

Elly shook her head. Who'd think a man would care that much about a wedding cake?

Before she retired for the night, Elly bent closer to the mirror to inspect her eyes in the dim candlelight. A few wrinkles shone beneath the soft light. Sighing, she dabbed cold cream at the corners of her eyes. This was no time to spare any hope of youthful glow. She smeared a wide swatch across her forehead and onto her cheeks. In the end, she looked more raccoon than woman.

Slipping into bed, she pulled the down comforter and quilts up under her chin, careful not to sully the bedding with her beauty cream. A familiar tap sounded on the window—three quick, two slow.

Bo.

Closing her eyes, she whispered. "Not tonight. I love Gideon. Love love love my Gideon."

But in spite of herself, she tossed the blankets aside, stepped to the window, and lifted the pane. "It's late," she whispered. "What can't wait until morning?"

He raised the lantern to her face. "Sorry, do you have a prior engagement with your woodsy friends?"

"Very funny." She consciously reached up to touch the thick band of cold cream. If this were Gideon, she would remove the balm. She

wouldn't want her soon-to-be-husband witnessing her nightly ritual until the time arrived, but this wasn't Gideon, and Bo had seen
her in every state—dirty, pretty, angry, happy. "What do you want?"

"Just passing by. Mrs. Pettit thought her time to pass had come.
She sent Doc to get me."

Elly sat up straighter. "Mrs. Pettit passed?" Why, they'd worked
on a quilt together earlier in the week. No one could beat Imogene's
stitching.

"No, she's fine. By the time I got there she was playing checkers
with the doc. Turned out she ate too much cabbage at supper." He
brushed a patch of dead needles aside and sat down on the ground.

"Please, make yourself comfortable," she said, hoping he noticed
the sarcasm in her voice. When he didn't move, she left the window
to wrap a quilt around her. When she returned, she was hit in the
face with a cranberry.

"Bo!"

"Shush. You'll wake up your pa." Bo flashed a grin.

She rolled her eyes. What happened to the men in her life? They
were acting like schoolboys. First Gideon's silliness with the Canada geese and now Bo with cranberries. She'd long left behind any
enchantment caused by such pranks. If Bo had stayed around, he
would have known that.

"I'm not keeping you up, am I?"

She shook the berry from her hair and chose an adult topic. "I
want your father to oversee the vows." She'd been worrying about
how to tell him, and a straightforward declaration seemed easiest.

Bo sat up straighter. "Pa? He's not a minister."

"No, but he's one of the finest men I've met. He's been like a second father to me, and I sincerely hope he will agree to marry me to
Gideon."

Light from the lantern revealed something akin to pain in Bo's face. The teasing was gone. "He will be honored, Elly. He's always loved you." He cleared his throat. "What does Holt think about your choice?"

"I haven't told Pa yet, but he'll be fine with the choice—once he cools down from the election." Elly hoped that would happen sooner rather than later. "Pa will be happy to walk me down the aisle. I'm going to be married here at the house."

He frowned. "Not the church?"

"In this house. That's my plan. Adele isn't happy about the choice. She believes the church is best, but I can't think of a better place than where I grew up. I wrote Ma about my plans. I know she'll agree. The vows will still be taken before God."

"This is yours and Gideon's choice to make." Finally, he said, "I like the intimacy of a home wedding."

A long quiet stretched between them.

It was Bo's turn to redirect the conversation. His words made cloudy puffs in the air. Elly tugged the quilt tighter. "I take it your pa is still worked up about Grover Cleveland."

"He's been on a steady dose of bicarbonate since the election. I've seen him like this before, almost every election cycle. He'll come around, eventually." She laughed. "Can you imagine if we'd married?" She couldn't believe she'd spoken the thought aloud. She quickly clarified the observation. "Every family supper, every social, and every chance encounter between Pa and Milt would mean hysterics. That kind of drama would get very tiresome."

He offered a knowing smile. "Their political disagreements never bothered me when I was young. Both are stubborn know-it-alls." He added softly, "I'm going to miss that ornery old cuss."

Bo must have been uncomfortable showing his emotion over his pa's health, so he changed the subject yet again.

"Do you remember the time we got in Pa's cabbage patch and

painted faces on six or seven heads? We left the things on Richardson's front porch."

Snickering, she nodded. "Adeline Richardson stormed out of the house in her robe intent on finding the culprits."

"She came to our house first," he noted. "Madder than a wet hen."

"Ours second."

"Did you fess up?"

"Me? I faked temporary amnesia," she said. "And you know, that could have been real when you shoved me out of that cherry tree."

"I didn't shove you out of anything. You lost your grip trying to kick me out of that branch. You couldn't stand it that I made it to the top first."

She lifted her right arm and pulled up the sleeve of her gown. "See this scar?"

Bo lifted the lantern. "No, I don't see anything."

Of course he couldn't see from such a distance, but she had a five-inch scar to prove her words. She tucked her arm back into the quilt. "That scar is as good as a signed note from you and that cherry branch."

"Speaking of signed notes, Miss Sullivan, you seem to overlook the times I took a switching for your pranks. I, however, have a perfect memory of being dragged into your root cellar to destroy jars and jars of beets, all because you didn't like their taste. When your ma came to investigate the noise, you hid in an empty crate, leaving me to take the blame. I didn't sit for a week."

Elly remembered the incident well. Gratitude still lingered in her heart toward Bo for all the times he'd taken the blame for her silliness. She knew she could always trust him to look after her. "But you didn't tell on me."

"I didn't. I wanted to, but I didn't." He met her eyes as he stood up to brush snow and dirt off his pants. "Just so you know, I wouldn't have performed the ceremony unless the Almighty came down and ordered me to."

Cold bit her cheeks. She was determined, this once, to speak her heart. "Just so you know, if you had agreed you would have broken my heart."

"I've already broken your heart...and mine. I'm sorrier than you'll ever know."

Lying in bed later, Elly wondered why Bo really stopped by. So far he'd kept a reasonable distance. They'd been able to talk like old friends.

Comfortable old friends.

Chapter 14

*Y*ou have to choose red, Elly. New Year's Eve is still officially the Christmas season and having a wedding at that time of year means you use red and green."

"I like blue. What's wrong with blue? You look lovely in blue and I know Gideon likes blue."

"Red, Elly." Adele jumped back when Rosie and Quint darted around the two young women who stood chatting in front of the mercantile.

Elly bit her lower lip at the couple's exuberance. Once she and Bo had performed the same crazy antics.

"Have you ever heard of blue flowers this time of year?"

"We'll use greenery. I much prefer greenery."

Dodging Rosie, Elly restrained her tongue. The two were acting like children. Thinking childhood crushes would blossom into soulmates.

"Got ya!" Bo yelled.

"Did not!"

Quint made a beeline between Adele and Elly and latched onto the hem of Rosie's skirt. The young woman squealed, her cheeks flushing a rosy red.

Her head filled with utter nonsense.

"There's still time to consider red." Adele shifted packages. "I'm thinking red with white trim?"

"What about baby blue—with white trim?"

"No, red is perfect. You'll see."

Whirling, Elly shouted at the couple playing tag. "Stop this instantly!"

Feet skidded to a halt. Rosie's eyes widened in disbelief.

"Quint, go home," Elly snapped. "Adele, we'll talk colors later." Taking Rosie by the hand, she led the bewildered girl toward her house.

"But...but..." Rosie sputtered. "What's wrong, Miss Elly? We were only playing tag."

"You're far too old to be acting like a child." Elly marched the girl off the planked sidewalk and across the street. By then her temper had subdued. She had no call to be so curt with the young couple, but the two chasing each other, their laughter...The sight brought back too many uninvited memories. Still, she should be more in control of her emotions. Her footsteps slowed. "I'm sorry, Rosie. I'm afraid I've taken my bad mood out on you."

"Oh that's all right, Miss Elly. I don't blame you. If Quint ever does to me what Bo did to you—well, I'll die. I'll simply curl up in a little ball and *die*."

Was her and Bo's separation the only news in Berrytop?

"No you wouldn't."

Rosie glanced up. "How can you say that? I would die if Quint grew up and rode away. Nobody wants to be a spinster."

Spinster! Elly held back a gasp. That's what the community thought, that she was doomed to be a spinster?

"That's ridiculous. I don't intend to be a spinster because I didn't marry Bo."

"But you don't want to marry anyone else—and I understand. I would *never* marry anyone but Quint."

"Life gets complicated, Rosie. Just don't pin all your hopes and dreams on one man."

"You did."

"And you see how that's worked out?" She hadn't meant to be that blunt, but Rosie should know that hopes didn't always come true.

"Is it because he's a pastor now? I heard you'd made him promise he would never be one, and now he is."

Was nothing sacred? "He made me a childish promise. It isn't his occupation that concerns me."

"You could be a pastor's wife?"

She could be a groundhog if it meant she'd have Bo back.

"You ask too many questions, young lady."

"Can I tell you something?"

"You may."

"If you ask me, I think he's still in love with you. Quint mentioned the fact the other day. You should see the way the pastor looks at you when you're not looking."

"Nonsense."

"It's true. He doesn't look at other women like he looks at you."

"He's a pastor. He can't look at other women disrespectfully."

"He's still a man, and he doesn't look at you disrespectfully. Just kind of sad like."

"You're mistaking friendship for love. Bo and I are still good friends."

"I don't think so."

"Well, I happened to know so. Now run along and tell your mother I said hello. I hope to see her at sewing circle next week."

Rosie walked off and Elly studied the child—flying hair, rumpled dress, soon to be a woman. *God, I pray that what she and Quint share lasts a lifetime.*

Spinster. The very nerve...

Shaking her head, she walked on.

Elly cringed when her bare toes touched the icy wood floor the next morning. Her breath made white puffs in the bedroom air. She knew without looking outside the first measureable snow had fallen. The house was bright with the light reflected by the sky's deposit. A quick look out the window revealed only a few inches on the ground, enough to outline the branches and fence tops in white.

So involved was she with the play of light in her room that she nearly missed the scent of cinnamon and yeast wafting up from the kitchen. She hurriedly pulled on warm britches and a wool shirt. If Pa awakened early and was putting his hand to cooking, she needed to step in before he burned the house down.

She breezed into the kitchen and stopped dead in her tracks. Her ma sat at the kitchen table. "Ma!" Flying into Irene's arms, she hugged her fiercely. "Why didn't you let us know you were coming?"

"I couldn't stay away another minute." Her hand cupped Elly's cheek. "I figured I'd beat any letter. When your aunt saw how anxious I was to get home, Milly insisted on sending me home on the train. Mercy, I thought the trip would never end. I arrived very late last night and didn't see the need to disturb you."

Elly renewed her embrace. "I've missed you so much."

"Coming home is the sweetest kind of goodness." She motioned to the opposite chair. "Sit. Tell me everything that's happened while I've been gone."

Holt wandered in with the scent of shaving cream in the air. When he bent to give Irene a kiss, Elly spotted a couple of remaining white spots behind his ears. "How're my two favorite ladies?"

Irene gave him a smile that warmed Elly's heart. Pa put on a gruff exterior for the outside world, but he loved her mother. Theirs was the kind of love she wanted, warm and enduring. They weathered bad harvests—sometimes two in a row—but never took their misfortune out on the other. Holt would spend the winter studying catalogues. By early March, his resilient spirit and unshakable faith sent him back into the bogs, eager for a new season, and Ma would be right beside him.

He looked to Elly. "I'm leaving it up to you to tell your ma about the wedding date."

"A wedding date?" Irene's eyes lit. "You didn't say a thing in your letters, but I should have guessed when you said Bo was back."

Elly fingered the lace tablecloth. "Not Bo, Ma. I'm marrying Gideon."

"Gideon?" Irene turned to look at Holt. "I'm a little confused."

"Bo is back, Irene, but Elly...I'll let your daughter tell you the details. Besides, this weather could take a turn for the worse, and I don't want to be caught empty-handed. I'm hitching up the wagon and heading to the feed store."

"Bundle up tightly," Irene called as he left the room. His voice echoed from the front closet. "Good heavens, woman, do you think I've gone daft in your absence? You think I'm going outside bare chested?"

After the door clicked shut, Elly filled her ma in on the particulars of the wedding. Ma took it all in, nodding her ascent to Milt's officiating. "And when is the date?"

"Maybe New Year's Eve. I want to marry in the parlor, wearing your dress. Gideon's an upright gentleman, Ma. I'm incredibly fortunate to have attracted his attention."

"Absolutely! He's a fine, fine man." Ma smiled, but a question in her eyes begged to be answered.

Elly knew exactly what she wanted to hear. She listed off all the reasons she wasn't marrying Bo, the ones she recited to herself daily. "He wants to be friends. He's a pastor, for heaven's sake. Too many years have passed. We've simply become different people with diverse hopes for the future."

Nodding, Irene's smile remained in place. "And you no longer are in love with him?"

Elly sighed. She couldn't hide the truth from Ma's searching eyes. "I'll always love him, Ma." Saying the words brought a deep ache to her chest. "But marrying Gideon is the right choice."

"Your pa seems quite impressed with Bo's new life, so not all the changes are bad, I suppose. For all of her waiting, I'm sure Faye must be very proud."

Elly rose to help herself to one of Ma's spiced cranberry muffins and a cup of coffee, all the breakfast she wanted.

"Adele's baby must be getting very near," Ma noted.

"After Christmas, about the same time as Anne's baby."

Ma shook her head in amazement. "Isn't that something? Milt and Faye will have more grandbabies than they know what to do with."

"They won't see much of Anne's baby. Her husband is moving the family to Oregon, where he's taken a new position with the railroad. They plan to put down permanent roots there."

"That's too far from family. Knowing Faye, she's already crying a river of tears over losing her daughter and grandbabies to the West." Ma seemed lost in thought. Elly prepared herself. Any pause in Ma's talking meant a difficult topic was about to come up.

"Let's go back to the wedding, shall we? There's always more to a girl's wedding than what little you've told me. I'm so glad I'm back to help. You've done a fine job with the house, and Pa says the harvest replenished our bank account. Let's make your wedding very special. What's left to be done?"

"Very little."

"That's interesting." She lingered over her coffee. Elly fidgeted in her seat. "Now, darling, I am touched that you want to wear my dress, but it's yellowed something awful. We have time to make a new one, just for you. The girls from the sewing circle have deft hands. I'm sure they would love to be a part of your nuptials."

Elly would never turn down a new dress, but all the fuss about a gown to wear one day of her life seemed silly and wasteful.

"I've looked at lots of patterns, Ma. They don't have any significance behind them. I hope Gideon and I can have half the marriage you and Pa have managed. Starting out in your dress will be most meaningful to me."

Ma's eyes welled with tears. "Oh, my. I'm very touched. Your pa will be honored too. Thank you, Elly. Your tribute is most welcome."

To lighten the moment, Elly returned to the former subject. "Sally Hawkins has agreed to make the cake. She'll frost it white and line the edges with pink rosebuds. I'm sure it will be lovely."

"Naturally, and Adele will be your matron of honor."

"Of course. Adele has been doing most of the planning for me. The harvest has kept me very busy."

Ma looked around the kitchen. Her smile faded. "We do have a good amount of cleaning to do before New Year's."

"Yes, the holidays always create extra clutter."

"I was referring to your wedding, dear."

"Oh. That too—if we decide on New Year's Eve."

"Dear...don't you think you should be choosing a date soon? The holidays are mere weeks away."

"Mmm."

The clock struck nine. They'd spent two hours catching up. Elly washed the breakfast dishes; Irene dried. Her ma had grown quiet again. In the weeks of her absence, Elly had forgotten Ma's ability to disarm her with a question. She scrubbed hard at the baking tin.

Irene bunched the towel in her hands. "Elly?"

"Ma." She knew the question before her ma asked. "We've already discussed Bo. I am not going to marry him."

"That wasn't the question. I was about to ask if you were in love with Gideon."

Elly took the towel from her to dry a plate. "Didn't Pa tell you where Bo has been or what he's been doing all these years?"

"We're back to Bo, are we?" She took the towel back. "Your pa only mentioned that Bo was back—that we would talk more about him this morning."

Elly filled her in on the sordid details of Bo's missing seven years. Seemingly shocked, Irene shook her head. "That doesn't sound like our Bo, not in the least."

"'Our Bo' was a bad boy, Ma, and the lifestyle suited him fine. He forgot all about his family, me, Berrytop, and the Lord. He was too busy looking for a good time."

Ma wiped at a clean plate. "Many folks fall away from God for a season and then return with even greater love for the Lord. Sometimes folks have to taste what the world has to offer to choose the Lord's love and reconciliation. They come back full force, like Bo."

"Oh, Bo's back full force. He even preaches a decent sermon." *Decent* was hardly a fair description of his messages. When he preached, folks sat up and took notice. She could admit that he now served the Lord as ardently as he had at one time served the devil. Perhaps Ma was right—for some it took a lost person's perspective to gain life-saving wisdom.

Irene scrubbed a skillet hard. "Having said all that, I can't help feeling for Faye. She must be fit to be tied. She raised her son in the church, taught him at her knee to love God and man."

"Church doesn't help a man if his heart isn't present." Elly knew all about missing hearts. Hers had been absent until Bo returned. And the deacon who preached the following Sunday followed Bo's lead. There was no shouting or pulpit pounding, only plain talk about God's goodness. Nothing quickened her faith more than Richardson taking to his sickbed. Folks even dared to speculate the Garrett boy might be persuaded to serve his home church and let Reverend Richardson take his long overdue retirement. The idea made Elly smile.

Turning from the sink, Irene took her daughter's hands in hers. "Darling, I love you with all my might. Whom you marry is one of the most important choices you'll ever make."

Elly dropped Ma's hands and returned to washing cups. "You're underestimating me. I've thought long and hard about what I'm doing."

"And you believe Gideon will be the man to love you when you're unlovable?"

Elly turned away. "No one person could be everything to a woman. Sometimes a person has to take happiness where they find it. Like you said, Ma, Gideon is a fine man. Please don't worry about me."

"Oh, honey." Irene reached out to draw her close. She held Elly tightly for a moment. Her words warmed her daughter's heart. "The day I stop worrying about you will be the day they lower me into the ground."

Chapter 15

Clouds parted to reveal a dazzling blue sky. Although cold, the day proved perfect for reconnecting with friends and neighbors before the winter cocooned the community.

Elly and Irene packed muffins in a basket and walked door to door to share the delicious treats. Elly could barely speak for the joy of hearing her mother laugh, pray, and recount memories with her long-time friends.

Late afternoon, the pair took notice of the fading light and, reluctantly, thoughts returned to home and chores. Elly suggested a quick stop at the mercantile for a couple staples before ending the outing.

Sitting on the outside bench, a woman wearing a cloak and bonnet sat motionless with a little girl whose cheeks blazed from the cold. Elly made note to check on the pair when they left the shop. They were new to town and could probably use a few directions.

Inside, they found the doctor purchasing pipe tobacco. Adele came through the door shortly afterward, and another round of welcomes enveloped Irene. Ma clearly enjoyed the attention.

Doc made Adele stand up front while he casually walked around her, assessing the baby's progress. "Dad gum if I don't think you'll be havin' that young'un early."

The expectant mother's face lit. "Honest?"

"Never know about these things." He winked. "He'll come when he takes a notion."

The hands of the clock inched toward five. Mr. Stack discreetly cleared his throat and the women broke apart. All knew Mr. Stack demanded a timely supper. They hurriedly made their purchases and stepped outside the store to say their goodbyes. Adele excused herself to clean the church before the evening meal.

"Aren't you too far along to be doing such work?" Irene asked.

"I go plum crazy if I sit around too much. I'll be a happier mama if I feel useful. Besides, I've cleaned the church forever and I want to pay the Reverend a short visit. The poor man seems to be going downhill."

With that, she pulled her cloak tighter and waddled off toward the parsonage.

The woman and child still sat on the bench. The woman gave Elly a hopeful glance when she exited the store. Were the two lost? Night would be here soon and cold was settling in. Elly bent to speak into her mother's ear. "Who is that?"

Irene glanced at the couple and whispered. "I don't know, but the woman and the child were on the train with me. I was so weary from all the delays I didn't try to make conversation."

The two women paused before the strangers. The woman raised her chin, a show of haughtiness. But the child leaned forward, eager for anything Elly could offer.

"Can we help you? Do you have someplace to stay?"

The woman sat up even straighter. "No, we're waiting for some-one. I knocked on the door, but nobody answered. I also left a note saying I would be sitting on the bench in front of the mercantile. So far, nobody has bothered to come."

Elly followed the woman's gaze across the road. "Someone will surely respond. The people of Berrytop are kindhearted. No one would willingly leave you out here in the cold. There must be some misunderstanding."

The little girl rubbed her arms and shivered, studying Elly with serious sky-blue eyes. Elly's heart went out to the child. Kneeling, she smiled. "I'll bet a hot meal and a crackling fire sound awfully good right now. Am I correct?"

The child glanced at the woman. The austere looking lady nodded sharply.

"Have supper with us," Irene invited. "We have plenty, and our house is nearby. We'll help find your friend tomorrow. Everyone knows everyone in Berrytop."

Indecision crossed the stranger's face. "We shouldn't move from where I promised we would wait. I'm sure our party will be along any moment." The little girl turned hopeful eyes back to Elly.

"Well then, who are you looking for?"

"Mr. Bo Garrett. Pastor Garrett."

Her answer was so shocking, Elly reached for the post to steady her legs. "Bo?"

The woman's features brightened. "Bo Garrett. Do you know him? Can you take me to him?"

Elly had heard gunshots in the woods earlier. Likely, Bo had taken the afternoon to hunt, since Milt's penchant for fried squirrel and biscuits still thrived. She glanced toward the Garretts' house where a light shone in the kitchen window. "We visited with Faye this morning. She didn't mention any plans. It's curious no one answered when you knocked. We can take you there on our way home."

"Thank goodness." The woman stood and reached for a small reticule.

As they walked through the crisply falling snow, Elly couldn't help but wonder about the woman. But more interestingly, who was the child? She lagged behind with noticeable weariness. "Walk with me." Elly extended a hand to the child. If needed she would carry the little tyke. "I'll take you to see Pastor Garrett." The woman stood straight as a picket, lugging a small bag and the reticule. Elly doubted she cared one lick about the child by her manner.

Approaching their back door, Elly shooed Ma and the little girl to the front of the line.

Pausing, the stranger noted, "Why, this is the house where I left the note." She eyed Elly suspiciously.

Elly frowned. "This is our house. We're the Sullivans. I'm Elly and this is my mother, Irene."

"I'm looking for Bo Garrett."

"Then you got the wrong house." Elly turned. "The Garretts live across the road. Come with me. Mother, you go in and get warm."

As the small party approached the Garretts, Elly detected the heavenly scent of pot roast in the air. Faye could make a roast that melted in one's mouth, served with rich dark gravy. Elly's stomach rumbled.

The threesome stepped onto the front porch and Elly knocked. Within seconds Milt answered the summons, his smile widening into a pleased welcome. "Elly. Come in, honey." His gaze swept the two strangers. "Who do you have with you? Come in, come in. It's cold as a well digger's boots out there. You look close to frozen."

The woman pulled the child by her coat lapel into the house. "Mr. Garrett? Bo Garrett?"

Milt's smile remained in place. "Bo's my boy. He's out back cleaning squirrel. Is there a problem?"

"My business is with him. If you would kindly retrieve your son, I would like to speak to him."

Milt glanced at Elly with a lifted brow. "Step in, ladies. I'll get him." He turned and left the room.

The little girl sidled closer to the stranger, almost burying her head in the lady's skirt. On closer inspection Elly saw the woman was not much older than she. She looked hard, like she'd lived a rigorous life.

Faye entered the parlor. "Oh good gracious, Elly. Take your things off and get closer to the fire. I fear it's going to be a bear of a winter."

The stranger restrained the child from eagerly accepting the offer. "Thank you, but I'll not be staying long."

Why this woman needed Bo so urgently was none of Elly's business, and yet the woman and the little girl fascinated her. Nobody came to Berrytop this time of year. Elly knew she should excuse herself and go home, but curiosity got the best of good manners. She wanted to know what that barely civil sourpuss was doing here. And a child that size should be home, eating a warm dinner and snuggling up with her favorite toy in front of a fire.

Faye gently eased the child from the woman's grip and settled her in front of the fire with a mug of hot cider. She spoke to the stranger as she unbuttoned the girl's coat. "Can I get you a cup of coffee, Miss?"

Judging by the mantle clock less than five minutes had passed, but time crawled. Why didn't Bo come? Surely Milt told him a strange woman and a little girl waited for him in the parlor.

Finally, the hinges squeaked on the back door and Bo's voice reached Elly's ear. He appeared in the doorway, drying his hands. "Someone need a pastor?" His attention focused on Elly. "Miss Elly."

His gaze then pivoted to the woman. "Is there something I can do for you?"

The woman stepped to where the child sat and pulled her up to stand before Bo. "I'm delivering Willow, and then I'll be on my way."

Bo studied the woman and looked back to the little girl. "Willow? What in the world are you doing here, darlin'? You're a long way from Parsons."

The child broke loose and ran to grab him around the legs. He bent and picked her up. Elly watched dumbstruck as a series of loud smacks exchanged. Bo knew this child. Knew her well.

"I brought her here on Jenna's orders."

"Jenna?" He frowned. "What's wrong with her?"

"She encountered an unfortunate...customer. She died during the skirmish. Her last words were, 'Take Willow to Bo.' It's been no small effort or expense to follow her wishes."

Bo's expression turned grave. "Jenna's dead?"

"Yes sir. Buried her two weeks ago." The woman reached into her pocket and then handed him a tiny silver locket. "She said someone else might enjoy this; the trinket had been the most special thing in her life." The women's lips drew tight. "She assured me you would reimburse me."

"Was she still working at The Soiled Dove?"

The lady found the grace to blush. "A woman's got to make a living, preacher."

Milt sank into his rocker, holding both hands to his head.

Bo studied the locket and then gently sat the child on the floor and placed it around her neck. "Of course. I'll get money for you." He turned, picked up Willow, and left the room.

Elly stifled a gasp. Her eyes flew to the child, comparing her features to Bo's. She didn't look a thing like him. His hair was dark, hers was blonde. In profile, the little girl's nose turned up. Her blue eyes were wide-set. The child's likeness must come from her mother.

Bo returned. Shaking his head, he spoke softly. "I'm much obliged to you for bringing Willow to me. I'm real sorry to hear Jenna is no longer with us."

"She's very shy," the woman said.

The child clung to Bo like a peach to a vine.

"Well, Willow girl." He looked at Faye. "Do you mind another mouth at the table?"

Faye's eyes glistened. "Not a bit." Mother Garrett's eyes held as many questions as Elly's.

"This young'un looks a mite hungry. Do you like pot roast, Willow Leah?"

The little girl nodded.

Elly lost all hope. He even knew the child's middle name.

"There's roast and potatoes. As soon as the biscuits come out of the oven, we'll sit down at the table." Faye smiled. She looked at the woman. "You'll be joining us, I hope?"

The lady shook her head. "My job is finished. I have a room in Madison. I'll be taking the train back to Dodge City in the morning."

"My sympathies." Faye smiled. "Bo, you ought to give her a little more money. The trains are a nightmare."

Elly stood mute as the scene played out before her. Bo had fathered a child.

Of the endless promises he'd made and broken, this one hurt the most. She found her senses to follow the woman out the door. Tears streamed down her cheeks.

Milt caught her by the elbow and whispered in her ear. "I'm deeply sorry you had to witness this, sweetheart." His kindness tore at her shredded heartstrings.

The revelation came at the worst possible moment. She had truly been starting to forgive Bo, to accept that mistakes were a part of life, and that he'd become a better man.

Now, the folly of her wayward thoughts made her cry harder.

Once again, Bo Garrett had played her for a fool.

Chapter 16

"Oh, Adele!"

The young woman jerked upright from polishing a pew when Elly burst into the church unannounced.

"What?" The cleaning rag dropped from her friend's hand onto the pew. Winter's fading light gave the church a sacred glow.

"He did it again!"

Adele moved faster than a woman heavy with child ought, her arms stretched out to embrace Elly. She pulled her into a pew to sit. "Quiet yourself. Who has done this terrible thing? Gideon? What's he done now? A pig? He's sent you a pig, hasn't he? I warned him to be more creative with gifts—perfumes, lotions..."

"Not Gideon, Bo!"

"Bo?" She frowned. "Bo's given you a pig? That doesn't seem like him, Elly. You're a promised woman."

Elly shook her head wildly. "He didn't give me a pig. It's what he's done, Adele."

"Oh my, what's he done now?"

"He sired a baby out of wedlock. A little girl."

Adele's jaw gaped. "That's not funny, Elly. We're in the house of God."

"It's true."

"Did Bo tell you this?"

"Of course not. He wouldn't tell me something like that." He'd know without a doubt the confession would hurl her to the edge of sanity. He'd disappointed her plenty already. And now this.

"Where is this child?"

Elly found it hard to breathe. "Here. Right here in Berrytop. At your house."

"A child just showed up? How did she get here?"

"Train."

Adele huffed. "Listen to me; I'm perfectly aware a child came by train. Tell me who brought her."

"A woman. A real grump. Not at all friendly, or the least bit tender with the child. She handed the little girl off to Bo and immediately left."

"And Bo accepted the girl?"

Elly's chin quivered. "Like a neighbor brought him a sack of fresh turnips. Just took the child and thanked the lady." She started to weep openly. "He even knew the little girl's middle name. Leah. Willow Leah. How many times can that man rip my heart out of my chest and stomp on it?"

Adele stood and paced. "Do you or do you not love Gideon?"

"I do love him!" She was sobbing now, sniffing and digging in her coat pocket for a hanky. "I just don't want to marry him."

There. She'd finally gotten the truth out. She breathed in and out slowly, trying but failing to regain composure. "I love Gideon but not the way I should."

The emotional dam finally shored up, and she drew a deep,

hiccupping breath and waited until her heart slowed down. "I thought you'd want to know," she said.

Sinking to the pew, Adele sighed. "You aren't making a lick of sense. If you came here to tell me you don't love Gideon enough to marry him, I think I already knew that."

"No, I came to tell you that Bo..." The dam burst and hot tears spurted fresh from her eyes. "Some other woman bore Bo's child. I would have doubted the truth if I hadn't seen him accept the little girl with my own eyes. His actions left no room for doubt."

Shaking her head, Adele scooted closer. She must have felt her own sense of disappointment with her brother, but she didn't show it. She pulled a handkerchief from her apron and traded out the one Elly had saturated. "Here. Try and settle down. Now, calmly, let's hear it all."

Drawing a deep breath, Elly clung to Adele's hands, willing the tears to stop. "Mother and I were coming out of the mercantile when we spotted a woman and child sitting on the bench. It was obvious they were waiting on someone or something, so we asked if we could help. At first the lady declined our offer, but then she asked if we knew Bo Garrett. We said we did and she said..."

Overcome, Elly buried her face in Adele's shoulder.

"Stay with me. What did the woman say?"

"That she was looking for Bo," Elly managed between sobs. "So we led her and the little girl to your house, and, lo and behold, it became clear the woman was delivering the child to him."

Slumping against the pew, Adele shook her head. "I feel sick." She covered her face with both hands. "How could he?" she whispered. "I cannot believe my brother would do that—especially to you, to my family. To God."

Elly tightened the embrace, their tears mingling. The lantern dimmed and the stove at the front of the church no longer glowed with heat.

Finally Adele released her and sat up straighter. "Were my parents there to witness this?"

"They heard everything. Faye was so kind and welcoming to the child, but clearly she was taken unawares."

The thought of Milt's gentle words as she fled the house brought fresh tears. After a bit, she sat up and wiped her nose on Adele's handkerchief. "The man doesn't deserve my tears." Elly lightly blew her nose and regained control. "And this little child will be a blessing to Faye when…" She caught back her next words. Adele couldn't know about Milt's failing health, not now before she was about to give birth.

It had been Elly's place to give Milt and Faye grandchildren, not another woman, not a saloon girl, for heaven's sake.

"Bo fathered a child out of wedlock." Adele repeated the words as though she was trying to somehow make them believable.

"He told me he sinned mightily," Elly whispered. "So I shouldn't be surprised." But she was. Staggered would be a better word. Felled. Flattened. How many ways could a heart be broken?

Adele slowly shook her head. "I don't believe it. Bo might have gone off course, but I do not believe he fathered another woman's child. He would not do that to you, Elly."

"But he did, Adele. I was the last person on his mind when he created this lovely child with another woman. I have to accept what I've seen with my own eyes."

"Unless he was in a drunken stupor, no one could make me believe he would do this. Elly, we have to believe he's still the man we've always known."

For a moment the women's eyes met. Both knew Bo drank and

caroused during the time he'd left Berrytop. He'd confessed as much to anyone who would listen—always quick to add the forgiveness he'd found in the Lord—so why would fathering a child be out of the question?

"Where's the child's mother?" Adele's question echoed softly in the darkening church.

"She's dead—something about a saloon brawl. The whole incident sounds like a dime-store novel, only a real little girl is without her mother."

Each new piece of the puzzle only seemed to indicate Bo's rebellious years would haunt him and Elly forever. It was hard enough to ponder what those years held, and even more devastating to stare into the eyes of the product of his youthful defiance.

"I am so sorry." Adele's eyes swam with unshed tears. "So very sorry his past continues to hurt you so deeply." She absently stroked Elly's hair.

Moments passed. Adele stood and added a log to the stove, adjusted the damper, and sat back down. "You know that you can't keep misleading Gideon. You have to tell him about your feelings."

Elly was tired of the ruse, tired of pretending, but most of all tired of deceiving herself. There wasn't enough cattle or manure in the world to make her love Gideon the way he should be loved. She couldn't keep leading him on when there was no hope for a real future together. "I know what I have to do. I've tried so hard to make Bo my past, to put him in his proper place in my life, but I can't. He meant too much to me. I'll go to my grave loving him, no matter what he's done."

"You need to tell him. Surely if you feel this strongly about him forgiveness will eventually come."

"I can forgive him, but I can't forget his past. And now there's a child involved." She sat up, touched the hanky to her nose, and tucked in stray curls. She hated to think how the crying reddened her nose and eyes. She couldn't go home until she composed herself. From this moment on, honesty was her new policy, especially when it came to matters of the heart. "Think of how I would have reacted to the child's sudden appearance if I had fully accepted him back in my heart. I could have forgiven him those years, Adele, but a child? With another woman? How would I have lived with that knowledge day in and day out, knowing he betrayed me to the deepest sense?"

"The child is an innocent victim. She had no say in this matter. She didn't have the privilege of choosing her parents. Would you honestly reject her?"

"No, of course not. I know she's without blame but—and I'm only being honest—I fear deep down I would resent her. I wouldn't want to, but it's possible."

"Acquiring a small child overnight isn't going to be easy on Ma and Pa," Adele murmured. "But we'll love her. If God chose us to raise her, then we will." The women sat in silence, focused on the cross that hung there.

"You know what Christ would do," Adele said softly.

"He welcomed all children, even when His disciples complained."

"Can we do any less?"

"It's easy for you to say, Adele. Bo's your brother. Your love for him is different than my love. God is absolute; I'm weak."

Sighing, Adele admitted. "I have no solutions. I just know that you can't marry Gideon, not with a halfhearted kind of love, and not when you still love Bo."

"Everything you've said is true, and you're a good friend for saying it. I've spent endless nights trying to find a solution. The thought of hurting Gideon a second time is unthinkable. Doing so would make me no better than Bo. Gideon's a wonderful person, but I don't love him the way a woman should love her husband. He's only a dear friend—or brother."

Adele's eyes widened. "Oh dear, I was afraid of that."

Elly clasped her hand. "Tell me what to do, Adele. I am so very confused."

Adele leaned closer and whispered. "I wish I could, sweetie. Our situations are very different, but I can tell you what I would do. I've lost a man I love, so my heart goes out to Gideon. I've lived in a lonely world without my love, and I wouldn't suggest you, or anyone, walk that road.

"This matter is between you and God. He tells us not to be unequally yoked. The Scripture is referring to matters of faith, but I wonder if the verse might include matters of the heart as well." She smiled to herself. "I guess the old adage is true: You can lead a horse to water, but you can't make him drink. A woman can marry a man, but the vow can't make her give what isn't there to give. Don't put yourself in that position, love."

Elly shook her head. "You're so wise, Adele."

"And you're so silly. I merely see things at this moment that you don't or can't."

"Where should I start? I'm so muddleheaded I hardly know my own thoughts."

"Well, to begin with, you must make up your mind about Gideon, permanently. You cannot keep toying with his heart and his feelings."

"I can't hurt him, Adele. I simply like him too much to hurt him."

Adele narrowed her gaze at Elly. "Well, then, make me understand how you think you're going to live with a man and bear his children without loving him. Do you believe that by marrying him and living a miserable life you will make him happy?"

"Gideon wouldn't make me miserable, Adele. He's kind and compassionate."

"So is Reverend Richardson. Would you marry him if he were available?"

Elly drew back in horror. "Never!"

"Then you, undoubtedly, will have a little trouble living with someone you don't truly adore. Living with a man you love desperately is taxing at times. Believe me, I speak from experience."

Elly shook her head. "How will I ever find the courage to tell Gideon these things?"

"If they need to be said, God will provide the courage." Adele sat back and rubbed her large belly thoughtfully. "And Elly, if you're lacking forgiveness in your heart for Bo, God will provide that too. All you need to do is ask. You have to be willing. What Bo has done seems unforgivable, but is it? Is one sin worse than another?"

Elly sat quietly absorbing the conversation. Bo had asked for her forgiveness and until tonight she thought she'd given it. She hadn't. His sins still ate into her flesh, numbing her soul, embittering her. Her punishment was even greater than his.

She sighed heavily. "Even if I could completely forgive Bo, he's never asked that we reconcile, not once."

"Perhaps he's more perceptive than we give him credit for. Perhaps he sees that you still harbor hurt and haven't truly pardoned him. Ma says the only person we hurt when we won't forgive is ourselves."

"I said I forgave him." She said the exact words, and meant them. Or thought she had.

"But you hadn't released him, not really. There's a big distance between our mouths and our hearts. We can say something and not mean a word."

"He could have told me he didn't believe me. He could have saved me a lot of hurt."

"Well, I'm not going to pretend to know everything about my brother or you, but I would guess the two of you are so attuned to each other's thoughts that he felt what you had given him were words, not your heart." She gripped Elly's hand. "Who has your heart, Elly? Bo or Gideon?"

Chapter 17

Who has your heart, Bo or Gideon?

Adele's words rang in Elly's head in the days following their conversation. All through polishing the banister and feeding the chickens and blackening the stove, Adele's admonition to fully forgive Bo played over and over. She'd never thought of herself as an unforgiving person, but she'd never faced this kind of distress before.

She rose from the table and dumped the remainder of her meal in the slop bucket. Food settled in her stomach like a rock.

She took her coffee to the parlor window to watch Willow play in the Garretts' front yard. The child worked with uncommon intensity to build a snowman. How she struggled to lift the middle section atop the base. Part of Elly wanted to don a heavy coat and mittens and help the child; the other part stood by to observe and wait for her heart to thaw. The town of Berrytop had no such struggle over Willow. The little orphan readily won the community's heart, and they accepted the child with surprising empathy.

Because of the bad weather, Gideon was preoccupied with his herd. He spent hours riding his property to make sure each animal had what it needed. Elly hadn't seen him in the past few days. He'd only commented on Willow with a sideways glance. He'd offered no speculation as to her parentage, and Elly hadn't encouraged the subject. Gideon and the community tampered their notice and their imaginations in deference to the Garretts.

Thanksgiving was one week away, and soon after, Christmas.

And then, the New Year.

Elly had done nothing more toward the approaching wedding other than spending an afternoon with Ma browsing the mercantile for material to make Adele's matron of honor dress, and even then she hadn't made a purchase.

The steam from her coffee cup rose, but she didn't drink. The activity going on outside the window proved more interesting than breakfast. Bo now played in the snow with his daughter. His little girl. A tizzy of envy and hurt boiled in Elly's gut and she felt the tug of rebellion. All sorts of other sensations boiled through her veins. She set the coffee on the table. Even laced with sugar and cream, the brew ate at her stomach.

Willow was a visible reminder of Bo's recklessness that had now come to affect so many, especially the Garrett family. Not one of them confirmed the notice aloud, but everyone knew the connection this child had to Bo Garrett. Of course he had to be the father. Why else would a dying woman send her child to him for life-long protection?

Willow's birdlike laughter penetrated through closed windows. Irene joined Elly in the parlor, carrying her mending to a chair by the window where the light was brightest. Elly knew she should return to the kitchen to wash the breakfast dishes, but the scene before her proved too entrancing.

Bo pushed Willow in a sled on the hard-packed wagon tracks on the road in front of their houses. Up and down the road he ran, encouraged on by the little girl's giggles. Elly tried to repress a smile, but a grin formed when she saw Bo wrapped around Willow's finger. That took no time at all.

She raised her eyes to take in the broad landscape of sky and fields and woods. Next year's cranberry buds were safely tucked beneath piles of protective snow and ice. The wood frogs now slept, frosted and still, in the woods beyond the Garretts' bogs; the ground squirrels huddled in their burrows; and the bunting and redstarts winged to warmer places. All would awaken and return come spring.

Come spring I will be a married woman...and possibly expecting Gideon's child.

Her gaze drifted to the box that contained her mother's wedding dress. She'd planned to take a nip and tuck here and there, but such busywork no longer drew her. Soon enough the days would be even shorter and drearier, perfect days for sewing duties. Absently, she reached for her coat.

"I haven't fed the chickens," she said. "I'll be back shortly."

Irene glanced up. "Dress warm."

With her gathering basket in hand, Elly stepped onto the porch, looking forward to reaching under the warm hens and listening to their noisy gossip. A fat snowball hit her square in the forehead.

Stunned, she dropped the egg basket, mentally sputtering. Of all the...

Her eyes easily located the culprit. Bo stood in the middle of the road, Willow at his side, grinning like a mule eating green grass.

Calmly kicking the basket aside and stepping off the porch, she reached into a drift to scoop up a mitten of wet snow and packed the wad tightly. She straightened to gauge the distance to her target.

Bo's grin widened as he bent to gather ammunition for his next salvo. Elly hurriedly mounded snow for a barrier. As they both prepared for battle, perfect calm settled on the snow and stirred the trees. Lazy white clouds crisscrossed overhead. The serene moment drew out and then curdled to crackling anticipation.

Snowballs flew, slamming into heads, shoulders, turned backs. Elly's squeals overrode Willow's as the battle intensified. She would not be beaten. A snowball smacked her cheek and tears sprang to her eyes.

As suddenly as the attack started, innocent fun turned to resentment. Resentment intensified into white-hot anger. Frozen balls flew through the air as fast as they formed. Bo staggered beneath the relentless assault. How could this man have destroyed a love that had been so perfect? How dare he!

Elly hurled the ammunition one after another until Bo curled into a ball in the middle of the road, arms over his head, fending off the attack. The harder she threw the more her tantrum built into an unrelenting charge.

Willow had withdrawn to the side of the house, watching with round eyes, apparently fearful she would be Elly's next target.

Finally, exhaustion overcame Elly. Sweat dotted her lip. She struggled for breath. She slipped to the ground, covered her face, and released the tears. She strained to name the source of her outburst. Certainly frustration, but acceptance? Had the unsettled nature of her future spurred the attack? She'd denied the truth of her feelings for months, but also wished without allowing herself to hope. Such contradiction demanded release.

She loved Bo. No matter how hard she tried to think otherwise, she loved this man with heart and soul. What did her misguided love say about her? That she was one of those impractical women who would forgive a man anything? She lifted her face to the sky. "Is that really what you want, God? Do you want me to forgive Bo for a vile and senseless act?"

A wind whispered across the frozen ground, and words formed

so clearly in her head she would have vowed they were spoken out loud. "I've forgiven worse."

She searched the sky for the source of the message. "But you're God," she whispered.

The answer came back distinct and loving. "Trust Me."

Covering her face with her hands, she dissolved into tears again. Her life swam before her—a life spent waiting to claim true love. She thought she trusted God, only to experience crushing betrayal. And yet, He asked her to trust Him even more. She didn't know if she could.

She slumped into a sobbing heap. She was barely aware of a pair of strong arms lifting her and holding her tightly. A familiar scent washed over her—wood smoke, wet wool, soap. She sought refuge in the base of his neck, her cries turning into painful heaves. A child's voice came to her. "Don't cry, Miss Elly. Bo won't throw any more snowballs." Willow turned to Bo and shook her finger. "No! No!"

Elly envied the childlike understanding of what just happened. She only saw the flying snowballs and the sharp smack when one landed. Elly knew the cause of her tears came from a deeper place. As tears do, these came from too many hurts and disappointments.

In the midst of her own turmoil, Willow's innocence and caring captured her heart. She could no longer resent such simplicity.

Bo nudged the Sullivans' back door open with the tip of his boot and carried Elly into the warm kitchen. Pa's sleepy voice came from the parlor. "What...? Who's here?"

"It's Bo and Elly," Bo called.

"And Willow!" the little girl added.

"Willow? Well come in here, short stuff. I think there must be a peppermint around somewhere. Irene, where's that candy jar?"

Willow broke away and ran in the direction of the voice. By now Elly had managed to gain control of her emotions. She sat at the table, unable to look Bo squarely in the eye. He must surely believe she had lost her mind—pelting him with snowballs, terrorizing him like an overbearing bully, and then sobbing uncontrollably.

He stepped to the stove and poured water from the steaming kettle into the sink. Adding cold water from the pump, he stirred the warm water with his hand. "Do you still keep the washcloths under the sink?"

He remembered that? He would. He was so...adjusted.

He drew back a curtain tacked to the counter, removed a cloth, and then dipped and wrung it out. Elly felt the warmth on her face, her cheeks, her hands. Bo's calming voice steadied her nervous tension. "I know you're angry with me, but did you have to knock my head off?"

Her cheeks stung with humiliation. She had no right to bludgeon him for any reason. And she surely didn't want to try to explain emotions she didn't fully understand. "I'm sorry. I don't know what come over me."

And that was the truth.

He rubbed a crimson splotch on the side of his cheek. "You throw a mean snowball, lady." Tossing the washcloth aside, he rubbed warmth into her white fingers, breathing on them to thaw their tips. Her soaked gloves lay in a puddle of melting snow on the floor.

She made herself meet his gaze. "Bo, I do apologize for my deplorable behavior. I didn't intend to knock your brains out."

"I hope not. I need what little I have left." They shared a hesitant grin. "You need to get out of those wet clothes."

"Yes, I will," she said. "Let me sit by the stove a bit more. We need something warm..." She started to rise, but Bo stopped her with a hand on her shoulder.

"Stay put." He turned, reached for two cups, and then poured hot coffee. Stepping to the back porch, he carried a pitcher of cream to the table. He also remembered how she liked her coffee.

Willow's voice drifted from the parlor, where she, Ma, and Pa were obviously having a big time. Willow's laughter and Pa's playful whinnies suggested they were playing horsey with Pa's feet. The memories of doing the same as a little girl warmed Elly from the inside.

"Giddy-up!" Pa exclaimed. Whinnies and snorts sounded from the parlor with plenty of laughter to follow. Elly marveled at the ease with which Pa engaged the girl with play. He exacted no judgment of the girl. That counted as a miracle at the Sullivan house.

Bo reached for a cold biscuit, stuck a piece of ham between the layers, and pulled up a chair. "So, want to talk about it?"

Elly took a fortifying sip of the steaming brew. "I said I was sorry."

"Okay. Now, let me go with you to see Gideon."

Their eyes met.

"You're not exactly in the picture anymore," said Elly.

"So you say."

"So I mean."

"No, I don't think you do," he said with the barest hint of a smile. "If the past few weeks have taught us anything, we both know that what we yelled that day from the pine tree stuck for life. I've checked. Our initials are still etched in the maple too. You can't argue with that kind of contract."

"Apparently, pledges and carved initials slide off you like hot butter."

"Touché."

"I'm not parrying with you, Bo. We loved each other then, and yes, I still love you. Deeply. But it's too late for us."

Bending closer he said, "What I'm about to say is completely inappropriate to say to an engaged woman, but it's true. We loved each other then and we love each other now. The question remains: What are we going to do about it? I've given you time, Elly. What I threw at you was hard to digest, but I knew that in time you could do it. You can't marry Gideon—oh, you could, but you won't. I know your heart, and you will never marry anyone unless you can give him all of you. You can only offer Gideon a life of service, not love."

Elly rose to pace. She needed to be clearheaded. "I don't want to grow old and die without a family. I want children and a husband who loves me like the young boy who stole my heart when I was so very young."

"That boy is sitting right here, Elly. Is it the same naïve young boy? Most assuredly not. I'm not without sin, but I am forgiven by God. I have no doubt about that."

Elly paused. The strange words she heard earlier flashed through her mind. *Trust Me.* "Bo, do you believe God speaks to some people?"

"Verbally speaks? Who can say? He's never spoken to me, but He's God and can do what He chooses. Why do you ask?"

She sat back down, fingered the rim of the mug. Someday, if given a chance, she would explain the voice—or sensation—she heard earlier. She took another sip of coffee. "It's odd how you can read me like a book."

"Meaning?"

"Meaning you're right. I can't marry Gideon. Maybe that explains why I totally fell to pieces earlier. I don't love Gideon the way he deserves to be loved. I've always known, but I thought it would be all right to settle."

"No one should ever settle. Why is it hard to wait until He shows the path? His time isn't our time." He surely sounded like a preacher, but Elly didn't mind.

"So I should just trust?"

He shrugged. "I didn't write the rules. But in order to forgive me you've got to forgive yourself."

"Myself? For what?"

"You feel you were a fool for believing in me."

His words tumbled around in her head. He was right; she'd hated herself for letting him go, felt like a gullible fool, when in truth she couldn't have stopped him from leaving that day.

"And there's God. You're holding a grudge against Him. Your life hasn't turned out how you planned or I planned. You think God betrayed you too."

Of course He had. God had taken everything she'd wanted.

"All of this is why I've held back, why I haven't said anything about the two of us until now. It's also why I encouraged you to marry Gideon. He is by far the wisest choice, Elly, but you won't do that to him. He's deeply in love with you. He would make you a fine Christian husband."

"But I don't love him. I love you." The words slipped out as naturally as a breath.

His eyes softened. "That's the problem. I've surrendered my life to God because I know His forgiveness is complete. I sense yours isn't, Elly. I don't blame you. I want to help you put your full trust in His forgiveness. The freedom that follows will change everything about your life. It's a gift, Elly. You can take it or not. If not, this oppression we find ourselves in will haunt us to our grave."

He searched her face. "I physically hurt with the need to live one more day of our youth, to hold you in my arms and laugh, to feel alive again with you at my side, but for now I rest in the knowledge of God's timing."

He hesitantly rested one hand over hers. Her hand disappeared under his. "I love you. I adore you. Every mixed-up crazy part of you, from your head to your toes. Nothing on this earth will ever change that fact. With all that is in me, I'm praying you can fully forgive me."

The sobering thought jarred her. Had she been angry at the God Richardson preached? Had she forgotten that even in His wrath upon a sinful earth, His love went far deeper? In His goodness and holiness, He forgave her. Would she ever fully commit to Him if she was incapable of extending that same grace to others?

Her fingers slipped between his and their hands locked tightly. Willow entered the kitchen and announced, "I'm hungry."

With a final squeeze, Bo left the table and scooped the little girl into his arms. "It's past your dinnertime. Let's go see what Ma has simmering on the stove."

Willow leaned into Bo's chest and beckoned Elly with a wiggle of her fingers.

"I can't come, sweetie." Elly took a final wipe at lingering tears. "But if you'll come over later, I'll have some fresh cookies coming out of the oven."

"Cookies!" She hugged Bo's neck.

Elly pushed back from the table and opened the door. Her eyes met Bo's. "I forgive you."

The warmth of his eyes melted her heart and asked a silent question. *Completely?*

"No." Honesty must be the first step. A slow smile spread across her face. If he couldn't see her white-hot love, he was hopeless. "I've decided to leave that up to God, but the two of us are okay now. I've made a few noteworthy blunders in my life—none as bad as yours—" She clamped down on the words. Full forgiveness was the goal. It wouldn't be easy to release anger some would call justifiable, but what choice did she have, especially when he had that same old Bo Garrett grin?

"You should think about having a serious talk with Gideon, and very soon," he whispered when he walked past carrying Willow.

Nodding, she wiped her eyes as he closed the door behind him.

Chapter 18

The thought of talking truthfully with Gideon made Elly squeamish. But she set her jaw and hitched up the buggy the minute the laundry had been scrubbed the following morning. She waved to Ma, who was sweeping snow off the front steps. Irene waved back and motioned for her to fasten the top button of her heavy cloak. Doing so, she blew Ma a kiss, climbed aboard, and slapped the reins against the horse's rump. The buggy lurched…and so did Elly's stomach.

An impeccable blue sky overhead did nothing to blunt a biting north wind. The cold needled her face, but the miserable ride to Gideon's fortified her for what lay ahead. She had prayed without ceasing during the long night. The thought of reuniting with Bo did nothing to lighten the task ahead of her. There was still much to consider, but she had a feeling that a love like hers and Bo's would always be there; nothing, including the worst, could break their ties. Her objective, honestly, was too difficult, but like a throbbing tooth she had to get to the root of her misery, and it wasn't going to be pleasant.

The door opened immediately when her shoes touched the wood

porch, and Gideon waved her inside as though he'd been expecting the visit. When she leaned to give him a peck on the cheek, he brushed off the greeting. "I thought you might come," he said.

"You did?" The statement surprised her. No one but Bo knew of last night's conversation, and she and Gideon hadn't planned a visit. The weather had turned too harsh for casual outings.

Moving to the stove, she teethed off her gloves and warmed her fingers. The house still smelled of ham and eggs. "I thought you'd be surprised to see me on such a miserable day."

"Not really. I've been expecting you."

She turned to face him. "You have?"

"Actually, I thought I might see you earlier this week."

"In this weather?" She should get to the point, but Gideon's demeanor confused her. "The horse lost his footing several times."

Gideon studied his feet. "Is that so? Perhaps you shouldn't have ventured out today."

She rubbed her hands. "Shall I fix us a cup of hot tea?"

His eyes rose warily. "If you'd like."

Puzzled by his short responses, she entered the kitchen and slid the teapot to the front burner, pausing to study the room. The back wall was dominated by the cabin's largest window. She stood at the sink to see a wide swath of snowy pastures, the barn, and corrals. Cattle pawed through the snow in search of grass. Footprints led down the snowy pasture to the watering trough, where Gideon had apparently chopped through the ice earlier. Being a cattle rancher demanded much of a man. A young bride, however, could keep track of her new husband from such a vantage point.

"Anything new at the homestead, Gideon?" she called. As a rule he would have followed her into the kitchen and chatted while the water heated. Instead, he remained in the front parlor. She spooned tea leaves into the basket.

The kettle sang, and she removed it from the heat and filled the teapot. Entering the front room, she set the pot on a table to let the tea steep before handing Gideon a filled cup. A red-and-white crocheted scarf stuffed behind a cushion caught her eye. She noted he stuffed the scarf further down into the sofa.

He took the cup. "Thank you." A rare silence stretched between them, giving Elly precious time to gather her thoughts and remember her carefully rehearsed lines. She had gone over and over her speech, praying she could make him see the wisdom of going their separate ways. No need to tell him of her conversation with Bo. Doing so would only heap additional hurt on the poor man. In time he would see that she wasn't simply fickle, but that she carefully considered their futures with mutual benefit.

"Gideon..."

"Elly..."

"Yes?" she allowed, gesturing for him to go first.

"About the scarf..."

Her gaze pivoted to the spot where she'd last seen it. "What about it?"

"It's nothing. Absolutely nothing. That's what I want to tell you. Cee's been stopping by and leaving pies and cakes. She must have left the scarf on her last visit this week."

"Visit?" Elly sat up straighter. "Cee visits weekly?"

"Sometimes more." He coughed. "Once in a while, she'll stay and eat. It's only polite that I ask, since she's brought the meal, don't you think?"

"Of course. Yes. That's nice of her. Well, as I was about to say—"

"You can't read anything into something so innocent."

"What?"

"There's no suspicious intent in Cee's bringing me food."

"No, I think it's very thoughtful of her." Especially since Cee lived miles away on the opposite side of Berrytop. It took an effort on Cee's part to make the visit. "Well, as I was about to say—"

"Because it's all perfectly innocent. You can't expect a woman to hurry off after a cross-country trip. We sit and talk a spell. You understand, don't you?"

Elly glanced up. "Understand?"

"About Cee?"

"Yes, I understand. She brings cakes and pies."

"Maybe an occasional casserole."

"A casserole? What kind?"

"Chicken and noodles. She brought some real tasty pork chops with all the fixings earlier this week. She makes a fine pot roast too."

Elly nodded. "She's an excellent cook."

"You should taste her gooseberry pie."

"I've had the pleasure at women's functions." Elly reached for her cup. The conversation was not going exactly as she envisioned. She checked her watch. "Gideon..."

"Because if bringing me food bothers you, I'll tell her to stop."

She frowned. Why should she worry about Cee bringing him food? She would have to thank Cee the next time she saw her. "Do you enjoy the dishes?"

"Very much," he admitted.

"I think it's nice of her to feed the bachelors..." Something about the word *bachelor* clicked. Cee hadn't mentioned a word about taking food to Gideon or any other single man.

"No." Shaking his head, Gideon got to his feet. "This has been bothering me for weeks now. Let me talk. It's not right, Elly."

"What's not right?"

"Cee and me. I enjoy her cooking."

She laughed. "So do I."

"No, I mean I enjoy her cooking...and her company. Somewhat. No, I enjoy her company a lot. So you say the word and I'll tell her to stop coming."

"I'm not going to tell you to stop enjoying her cooking. That would be senseless. Cee loves to cook, and I'm glad you enjoy her thoughtfulness."

He shook his head harder and paced like a caged bear. "It isn't right. I wouldn't want another man coming to see you five nights a week."

"Five nights? I thought you said she came occasionally."

"Five nights isn't like seven nights."

"No. Five nights isn't seven nights." For what it was worth.

"Her gooseberry pies are the best around, but if it hurts your feelings, I'll put a stop to those too."

"Gideon, I don't care if Cee brings you meals. I'm here this morning to..."

His pacing ceased. "Are you saying that you don't give a fig if Cee feeds me?"

She stared at him. "I don't give a fig, Gideon."

"Now I've hurt you, haven't I? That is the last thing I wanted to do—hurt you. I am so sorry."

"You haven't hurt me. It's dinner, Gideon, not poison ivy."

She eased to the front of her chair, trying to understand his consternation. She was the one supposed to be hurting him right about now. Instead, she was consoling him over some chicken and noodle casserole.

"I can't tell you how happy I am you feel like this."

"That Cee brings you food?"

"Yes."

"Got it."

Clasping a hand to the back of his neck, he resumed pacing. "Because the last thing I want to happen is for us to break up over a silly thing like another woman bringing me a casserole."

"Break up. That's what I want to—"

"Okay. Okay! I understand. I'd feel the same way, if I were you. We've been engaged twice, and what would it look like if we broke up a second time because of some needless misunderstanding about Cee and me? Granted, we've been seeing each other—not on a personal basis—but she does bring a meal and we talk. There have been occasions when we've taken long walks back to the wooded area. It's real pretty there, even in the winter. The snow catches on the branches and well, it's nice. We even sit on the porch and watch sunsets. We had to wrap ourselves in quilts last night. I didn't know I enjoyed walks in the woods and watching sunsets. She's an interesting conversationalist and loves cattle farming too. Did you know her grandparents were part of a party that crossed the Continental Divide? Imagine that."

"And she makes good chicken and dumplings too," Elly guessed.

"Yes! Did she tell you?"

"Lucky guess."

"She's funny and she loves kids. She says she wants a houseful. A cattle ranch can use a lot of children, what with herding and mending fences and milking."

"Really?" Elly sat back and allowed him enough rope to finish hanging himself. He was dumping her for Cee.

"You're absolutely right, Elly. Maybe we—me and you...maybe..."

He needed help. "Aren't meant for each other?"

He whirled. "That's it. We're not right for each other. You're a fine lady..."

"Who detests cooking," she helped.

"I thought you might improve."

"And what do I know about cattle? I've been raised in cranberry bogs. Cranberries and cattle. They don't match."

"Exactly!"

She shrugged. "It's possible we should call the whole wedding off. We've gotten very close to the altar before and something always intervenes..."

"God. God intervenes," he said.

"Yes."

"So you're all right with us seeking our happiness elsewhere?"

"Breaking up? Yes." Pursing her lips, she said, "It's a painful decision, but a wise one. The right one. Thank you for seeing what I'd refused to recognize."

He dropped to his knees. "What a relief. You don't know how I've worried and prayed about this. I don't want to hurt you, Elly. You're the last person on earth I want to hurt, but somehow, Cee seems so right for me."

Elly didn't have the heart to tell him why she'd come that day. Why heap misery on top of what seemed to be genuine happiness, especially when the outcome was the same? God did work in mysterious ways when left to His own methods.

Gideon quickly gathered her coat and gloves. "I'm so relieved we had this talk." He helped her into her warm coat. "I have a piece of Cee's gooseberry pie left. I'm going to wrap it and send it home for your lunch."

"Thank you." Elly determined to give the pie to Pa. Even though the conversation had had its happy conclusion, she didn't have the stomach for Cee's pie anymore.

He left and was back in minutes carrying a wrapped bundle. "Enjoy the pie." He opened the door and ushered her out, firmly closing the door behind her.

Standing alone on the front porch, Elly felt as though she had been felled by grace. God's incomprehensible compassion flattened her, in a very lovely way. She allowed every worry about her encounter with Gideon, every mumbled rehearsal of apologies and explanations, to evaporate into thin air.

Stepping down, she hummed "Amazing Grace" all the way to the buggy and then all the way home.

Chapter 19

$\mathcal{E}$lly nudged the horse to a faster clip. She sang a marching song and encouraged him on with hip-hips, just as Pa taught her. A burden had been lifted, chains broken, her heart lightened. The cold no longer needled. Winter's bite enlivened her to renewed possibilities. She allowed herself to think of other mornings like this, of the fire in the stove warming the kitchen, of her and Bo sharing a late-morning coffee.

The buckboard rattled into the Sullivan yard. Elly drove the horse to the back of the house to the barn and braked. She whirled toward the sound of Faye Garrett's screams.

Jumping down, she raced around the corner of the house. She expected to see that Old Jake, the community hound, had cornered Bo's mother near the front step. He'd become more of a menace as winter deepened. Instead, Elly saw Milt Garrett lying in the snow near the smokehouse, a shovel beside him. Faye knelt in the dirty drifts, calling out his name. Her shoulders heaved with sobs.

Sometimes at the most unexpected times, life strikes with a rattler's vengeance.

Bo rounded the house and Adele stepped on the porch, called

there by their mother's cries. Bo raced to his father as Adele carefully maneuvered the porch stairs as fast as her swollen body would allow.

Bo bent over Milt's form, checking his neck for a pulse. His head dropped to his chest and he stood and gathered his mother and sister into his arms and held them close. The family's mingled sobs carried over the brittle landscape.

The front door opened, and Willow ran out of the house to the fallen man. "Papa!" she cried. The wind picked up her innocent words and carried them to Elly. "Get up, Papa. It's cold." The little girl tugged at the lifeless arm until Bo reached down and scooped her up.

The community flooded the Garrett home with edible tributes in the following days—cakes, pies, casseroles, meats, bags of vegetables, and loaves of freshly baked bread—all offered to assuage pain. Not one mourner thought to say Milt had gone to a better place when he loved the Wisconsin countryside and his family so openly. A pall hung over the small community; preparations were made and a fresh grave dug in the small family cemetery.

God shone on the Garrett family when He sent three calm, snow-free days in which to bury Milt. Friends and loved ones gathered beneath a copse of trees as the sun rose over the bogs.

Gideon stood beside Cee on the morning of the service, his arm supporting her as she cried softly. If anyone wondered about which lady he should have been comforting, no one voiced their puzzlement.

Elly hovered near Bo, Faye, Adele, and Willow. Anne had not been able to travel, too great with child to make the long journey. Elly was mindful that standing too close would be seen as out-of-place and inappropriate, but she didn't want to be too far from Faye if grief overwhelmed her during the service. Bo supported his stoic and proud mother as the light breeze lifted her dark cloak.

When the assembly gathered close, Bo stepped to the open grave, holding a piece of paper his father had written and handed him weeks earlier. Elly doubted there was a hint of moisture left in Faye's tiny frame.

Clearing his throat, Bo opened the service with a short prayer and then began. "Pa said he didn't want a big fuss when this day came. He instructed me to read this particular Scripture when we laid him to rest and then tell everyone to go home. He didn't want anyone getting frostbite."

Reverend Richardson shuffled and huffed. Elly knew how it pained the man to endure a short service. She bit down hard on her lip to control an unexpected smile. Richardson would have them stand until their feet were frozen to the ground, reciting Scripture after Scripture. And then he'd point his stubby finger at all in attendance to tell them a funeral was a wake-up call best heeded.

Bo opened his Bible, but he didn't look at the page as he recited.

> Blessed are the poor in spirit: for theirs is the kingdom
> of heaven.
> Blessed are they that mourn: for they shall be
> comforted.
> Blessed are the meek: for they shall inherit the earth.
> Blessed are they which do hunger and thirst after righ-
> teousness: for they shall be filled.
> Blessed are the merciful: for they shall obtain mercy.
> Blessed are the pure in heart: for they shall see God.
> Blessed are the peacemakers: for they shall be called the
> children of God.

> Blessed are they which are persecuted for righteousness'
> sake: for theirs is the kingdom of heaven.
> Blessed are ye, when men shall revile you, and perse-
> cute you, and shall say all manner of evil against
> you falsely, for my sake.
> Rejoice, and be exceedingly glad: for great is your
> reward in heaven: for so persecuted they the proph-
> ets which were before you.

Kneeling, he scooped up a handful of earth and sprinkled it over the casket. "See you soon, Pa." Stepping away from the gaping grave, he reached for Elly's and Willow's hands.

⟨≁⟩

With the weariness of grief heavy on her shoulders, Elly leaned on the kitchen sink and washed the last plate later that evening. Ma and Pa hosted a light supper for some of the churchgoers who had attended the funeral.

The guests lingered with her parents in the parlor, reliving memories of Milt and his delightful sense of humor. Although the thought of socializing only added to her weariness, Elly loved to hear the stories of happier days.

Lawrence Simms's energetic voice sounded. "Remember the time when ol' Milt pressed you into a wager that he could run five miles and never flinch? You full remember that you showed up in long johns, ready to prove yourself tougher than Milt. The two of you agreed the monies would be given to the church.

"As I recall, you two thought the joke was private. You were both mightily surprised by the turnout on a bitterly cold morning. I do believe the whole community was there to witness the spectacle.

Why you picked sunrise, I'll never know. I nearly froze to death myself with two coats and a muffler. You both stood hopping and slapping your shoulders to keep warm until someone yelled out to get going. Red-faced but good-natured, the two of you made it across the finish line. Funny, but I don't recollect who won."

Pa said softly, "Milt, who else?"

As they exchanged stories, laughter, at first guarded and then enthusiastic, sounded from the parlor.

Elly couldn't imagine a world without Milt. In her heart, she spoke to him: *I wish there had been time to tell you that Bo and I are mending fences. That there's hope for us yet.*

The busyness of death left no private time for her to talk to Bo. How she longed to fly to him, to take him in her arms and kiss away the sadness in his eyes.

A snowball hit the window.

Sighing, she wondered why the love of her life couldn't knock on the front door like everyone else. Lifting the window, she called, "You knocked?" Her gaze settled on his outline in the winter's moon and her pulse thrummed. She didn't care if he threw boulders; he was always a welcome sight. She eased the glass open a bit more. "Bo, come closer."

Seconds later he stood at the window. Shivering, she rubbed her arms. "Goose, why didn't you come in?"

"I was about to, and then I thought, I don't want an audience for this."

The solemnity in his voice quickened her pulse. He was here to tell her that whatever had taken place a few days back had been a mistake.

She summoned the courage to say, "Whatever you have to say, say it."

"Well, now you sound downright unfriendly." He moved closer to the window, removing his hat. "I heard an ugly rumor that you and Gideon rethought your engagement and decided to drop it."

"Yes." She sighed. "I wanted to tell you, but I haven't had a moment alone with you. I went to Gideon's the morning after..."

Words trailed when his arm reached through the open window and drew her closer. "You're going to have to get closer. I don't want to scream this, but I will. "

Offering a shy grin, she taunted, "I can hear from this distance."

"Come on, Elly, I don't want to disturb your parents and their company."

Everyone would know who said what by morning anyway. Nothing was sacred in Berrytop, including private conversations. Just the same, a girl couldn't be too careful. "You'll have to wait a minute if you want to talk to me properly."

She closed and locked the window. Bo looked positively crestfallen. Elly didn't linger. She rushed to gather her coat and mittens and stepped outside to meet him, leaving the door open in her haste. "You have something to say to me?"

Drawing her slowly to him, he whispered, "Just wanted to be friendly. Hello, Elly." Her eyes drifted shut and the exquisite touch of his mouth closed over hers.

The kisses came softly, and then hungrily. Years peeled away and she was hopelessly lost in his embrace, both ecstatic and needy. Bo was no longer a young boy. He was a man, and she was a woman.

She wrapped her arms around his neck to pull him closer. She'd waited for this moment longer than she cared to remember. Even her dreams focused on this time and place, and she didn't care if curious eyes were staring out the back window.

Bo was finally home.

Breathless, they kissed, each encounter growing longer and more urgent with hasty snatches between breaths, minds crying, *I love you. What took you so long to surrender? I can't hold you close enough.*

She had no idea how long the embrace would have lasted, if Ma hadn't made herself and the others known.

"Good heavens! What is the back door doing open? It's winter..." Ma paused with her head half out the door. Once she'd taken in Bo and Elly's embrace, she disappeared and closed the door quietly.

Far too soon, Bo pulled back but didn't completely release her. He clung to her with the desperation of a drowning man, and she held him, knowing this was his way of releasing his pain. For three long days he'd carried the crushing loss of his father. He'd lost the man who watched him born into the world, seen his first step, helped pull his first tooth. Milt had taught him how to set a hook and flush out game in the woods. Milt taught him to ride. He took Bo to the woodshed when needed and shared an abundant measure of unconditional love afterward. Milt made Bo the man he was today.

Now, grief poured out of Bo Garrett. In Elly's arms, his shoulders heaved and she drew his face to her heart. Hot tears rolled down her cheeks as pain rolled out of him. A barn owl hooted from a nearby tree, but no other sound touched the night.

They were together now. Bo was right where he belonged.

Chapter 20

Turning off the lantern, Elly crawled beneath the covers with morning only a few hours away. Saying goodnight to Bo had been difficult. There was so much to catch up on, so many misunderstandings to clarify. Elly laid her head on her pillow, blanketed by peace.

She'd come to anticipate bedtime as a time to continue the heart-to-heart talk she'd started with God. The way Bo talked about Him made His presence so much more real. And His grace? Knowing all of her sin had been paid for in full and secured her a place in eternity made her love God even more. Not only that, His blessing extended to her in the here and now. He'd been faithful and brought Bo back to her, a little damaged and worn, but better from his experiences.

In a way, she was thankful for the years of Reverend Richardson's teaching. Although he hadn't presented a full picture of God, she appreciated a loving God, chock-full of grace and mercy, all the more for the contrast.

Settling beneath the blanket, she said softly, "It's been a good day, God. I know Milt is resting in Your eternal love. Comfort Bo, Faye,

Adele, and Anne. Give Faye more strength than she'll need for the coming days—"

Something hit the window.

Her bare feet touched the frigid floor in seconds and the window sash flew up. Bo was back. "Don't you ever sleep?" she teased.

He twisted his hat in his hands. "Willow isn't in her bed."

Elly sucked in a breath. "It's past two in the morning."

"We've looked everywhere. The barn. Under her bed. Every closet and pigeonhole in the house. We've checked every cellar and out-building. She's nowhere to be found."

Blood turned to ice in Elly's veins. The warmth of her bed faded. Above her, the black sky was crystalline. "I'll get dressed." Closing the window, she hurriedly discarded her gown for long johns, britches, and a wool shirt.

Within twenty minutes—a very long time for a young child to be out wandering on a winter's night—the able-bodied had been woken to join the search, and the good people of Berrytop, for the second time that day, had come to support the Garrett family.

Lantern light bobbed across the frozen landscape as groups of searchers spread out across the bogs and fields. Elly led one of the groups, mostly men, through a thick pine grove. The trees' bare branches cast grotesque shadows across the snow and gave her a sense of foreboding. She dismissed the thought and said a prayer for Willow's safe return.

Within an hour, Elly's teeth were chattering and she could no longer feel her toes, although she wiggled them wildly inside her boots. All around her, she heard searchers calling the girl's name. Sweeping the lantern for tracks yielded nothing except rabbit and deer prints. The thought of continuing the search washed her with fatigue, but giving up was not possible. Willow was too precious and vulnerable.

The sky lightened to charcoal and then to the color of a mourning dove's feathers. The searchers looked behind every fallen log and under every bush for hours, and still Willow had not been found.

Two parties met up, soon joined by three others. "Well," someone said, "I can't say what to do. We've looked everywhere but the river, and it's frozen solid. I don't see how she could have fallen through. If anyone's willing, I'll take a party to search from the bridge to where the river joins the creek. I don't expect to find her there."

Bo shook his head. "A party has been up and down the river, but thanks for your willingness to press on, Fred. I have no idea where else to look."

Faye insisted on joining the search, and nobody had the heart to deny her. Everyone understood the need for distraction in grief. She added a sense of clarity to the discussion. "She's been incredibly upset about Milt all day. She hasn't eaten a bite since yesterday. She's done nothing but look out the window. It's like she was looking for him. I can't help but think she's closer than we think. You searched every inch of the barn?"

"We have, Faye. If you want, we'll retrace our steps," a neighbor offered.

The widow shook her head. "Why don't we go back to the house? I'll make breakfast and some hot coffee. Once we thaw out, we can make a new plan."

When others turned back, Bo stayed put. Faye turned to look over her shoulder. She beckoned him. "Don't be stubborn, son. You can't do any good out here if you're frozen solid. The sun will clear the trees in half an hour. Our chances of finding Willow will improve with morning."

Elly sidled up to Bo. "She's right, Bo. In half an hour we'll be able to spot her tracks."

Bo appeared to hear, but he was obviously deep in thought. "Did anyone check Pa's grave?"

Elly shook her head. "Not that I know of." With a quick survey of the search parties, it turned out no one had been eager to walk in a graveyard in the black of night.

Bo turned and ran toward the family plot. Faye shouted after him. "Bo, the child could be anywhere! Come home and get warm." She turned to Elly.

"I think Bo might be on to something. It's worth a try."

Before the idea was fully formed, Elly whirled and raced after Bo.

Breathing hard, Elly raced toward the family cemetery. Bo was well ahead of her, calling, "Willow!"

"Willow!" Elly echoed.

"Where are you, girl?"

"Willow, answer me!"

"Willow!" Bo unlatched the gate enclosing the seven Garrett graves. The soft light of dawn revealed six graves and one fresh one. Elly wiggled through the gate behind him. Willow lay on top of the fresh grave. Jake, the old farm dog, lay beside her to keep sentry.

Holding up, Elly bent with hands to her knees to catch her breath. The frigid air burned her lungs. "Bo, is she all right?" She braced herself for the answer.

Bo stepped into the soft dirt and gathered the child into his arms. "Good dog, Jake. Good boy."

The dog whined. His tail thumped on the fresh dirt.

Willow stirred. "Cookie?"

"Here." Elly stripped out of her coat. "Cover her with this."

The child snuggled into Bo's collar. Her words came soft and halting. "Papa won't come out."

Bo added his jacket to swaddle Willow's body. She never would have survived the cold had she not been wearing her coat. Now, she wore three.

"Let's get her warmed up."

Chapter 21

Bo's long-legged stride covered the frozen ground. The weariness of a sleepless night enveloped Elly. She lost ground behind him, but she pressed on.

Willow stirred under the coats. "I cold."

"I know, sweetheart," Bo said. "We'll be warm in a few minutes. And Grandma is making breakfast. I hope you're hungry."

How about that? Bo had already adopted the child as his own. The thought of an instant family warmed her.

As they approached the house, men filed out of the house as if someone herded them with a stick. Bo deposited Willow before the fire and recruited a man to rub warmth back into her feet.

The women gathered in the parlor, chattering and chirping like a clutch of hens. Bo stepped into the circle of women warily. Looking for his ma and not finding her, he called out. "Ma? What's going on?"

Faye streaked through the parlor carrying an armload of white sheets. "Adele's in labor. Can you imagine?"

"In labor? Now?"

Faye turned toward the stairs. "Come along, Elly. You're needed upstairs." She paused and turned toward Bo. Tears filled her eyes. "Oh my goodness, I forgot to ask about Willow. Is she all right?"

Bo put a hand to her shoulder. "She's in the kitchen getting her feet rubbed."

A cry sounded from upstairs.

"We'd better see to Adele," Faye said.

Elly spoke to Faye's back, "The baby isn't due for another few weeks."

"Tell the baby, not me." Faye called over her shoulder to the women downstairs. "Better set the kettles to boiling."

When Elly saw her friend, red-faced and glistening with sweat, she stopped at the doorway. "Goodness, what a day." Everyone seemed to know what they were doing. One woman helped Adele out of bed while Faye spread fresh sheets. She felt like an extra wheel on a wheelbarrow. "What can I do?"

"If you want to be here when the young'un is born, you'd best step inside the door," Faye said. "Take the end of that sheet and tuck it into the mattress."

Elly had promised to be by Adele's side when the big event took place. She hadn't, however, prepared herself to see her friend in such discomfort. But when Adele looked at her with great relief, Elly hurried to her side.

"Oh, thank goodness!" Adele propped on her elbows, her eyes squeezed shut against a building contraction. "Where have you been?"

"Out searching for Willow."

"Tell me you found her."

"She's being cared for downstairs. There doesn't seem to be any lasting—" Elly broke off when Adele motioned for her hand. Adele's grip turned viselike. As the wave subsided, Adele fell back into the pillows.

Elly wrung water from a cloth into a bowl and rested it on Adele's forehead. She had no idea if the diversion helped a woman in labor, but she felt compelled to do something.

Faye hovered nearby. "Take deep breaths, dear. The doctor will be here shortly."

When another pain overcame Adele, the young woman cried out. "What's taking him so long?"

Faye spoke evenly. "He's been summoned. He needed to change into dry clothing and eat a bite of breakfast."

"He helped search for Willow," Elly said.

"Eat? The man is eating while I'm having a baby?"

Elly kissed the mother-to-be on the forehead. "Relax. You have plenty of time."

Adele's eyes widened. "This is going to go on a long time?"

Tsking, Faye straightened the twisted sheet. "One never knows how long birthing will last."

Another spasm hit and Adele twisted Elly's hand until tears smarted to her eyes. Elly glanced at Faye.

"It could take all day, dear." Faye reached to pat Elly's shoulder. "Go keep Willow company."

Elly located the child in the kitchen surrounded by motherly hands. For the first time, she was able to take the child in her arms and give her a firm hug. "You scared us, Willow. Please never leave the house without telling someone."

"Papa."

"I know. We all miss your Papa, sweetie." Filling the teapot, she set it to boil. "Want some more milk?"

The child shook her head. Eyes drooped.

"You're very tired. Why don't I give you a warm bath and put you to bed?"

At the mention of bed, the girl's strength returned. "No!"

Elly sat down at the table and stared at the child. She was slowly creeping her way into her heart. Love would not be hard to find. She could easily raise this girl—give her love and a good home. She could overcome the past if it meant a life with Bo.

Sighing she smiled. "You have a good daddy. You are very blessed."

Willow shook her head vigorously. "Bad daddy."

"Willow!" Elly sat upright. "Why would you say such a thing? Your daddy is very good."

A sly grin crossed the child's features as though Elly was teasing and she'd caught on to the jest. "Huh uh. He's bad man." Willow spooned applesauce into her mouth.

Elly glanced over her shoulder, praying Bo wouldn't walk in and hear her talking like this. Wiping a stray drip of applesauce, Elly lowered her tone. "You must never let your daddy hear you talk this way. He's a good man, not bad."

"Snake," Willow pronounced.

"Your daddy is a snake?"

Big eyes turned on her. "Mommy says Daddy lives in the grass."

Elly felt faint. What had her mother told her about Bo? No, he was not the model of sainthood, but he certainly would never hurt Willow and he wasn't a snake.

Suddenly Willow's words hit her.

"Willow? What is your daddy's name?"

"Buck." She dug for another spoonful of applesauce.

"I thought Bo was your daddy." The faintest hint of an all-out miracle started to form in Elly's mind. Out of the mouth of babes...

Again Willow looked at her as if she'd turned daft. "Bo's my friend, silly."

"And Buck would be..."

"Daddy."

The low-down snake-in-the-grass who undoubtedly sired this

little angel and walked away from her mother. Children's ears could pick up the important information.

Springing to her feet, Elly squealed, grabbed the child up from the chair, and smothered her face with grateful kisses.

Giggling, Willow wiped the kisses away. "Play?" she asked.

"You can play—you can do anything you want!"

Setting Willow on her feet, Elly did a jig around the room, dancing her way past the expectant ones who waited for Adele to give birth, past her pa who stared at her as though she'd grown horns, and out to the front porch. She located Bo walking back across the street with the doctor.

Coming to her senses, she cleared her throat and made some sort of an apology to the gathered neighbors.

Bo wasn't Willow's daddy; Buck was.

In deference to Adele's child's pending birth, she would wait to tell Bo.

She glanced at her watch. As long as the baby didn't take too long.

The collection of women downstairs thinned and disappeared through the morning hours. Bread needed to be baked. Roasts put in the oven. Laundry scrubbed and children tended. Adele labored on.

Every thirty minutes Faye and Elly switched places. The doc had arrived shortly after nine. The baby might be early, but it was in no real hurry to make an appearance.

Around eleven, Elly escaped to the front porch, where a group of single girls gathered to support Adele. Elly shook her head when questions flew. No, the baby wasn't here yet. Yes, Adele was doing fine. "The screams only make it *sound* as though she's dying."

No one seemed comforted by her explanation.

Accepting a mug of hot coffee from a neighbor, Elly thanked her and sat down beside Bo on the steps. Cold seeped through her bones. "Why isn't everyone inside?"

"It's a little noisy in there." He reached to draw her near. "I noticed Gideon standing beside Cecelia at the service."

Stifling a yawn, she nodded. "I haven't found a moment to tell you. Gideon and I had a very long, very unusual talk."

"How did he take the news?"

How did he take the news? Apparently well. "Good."

"Good?" Bo shook his head. "I figured he would put up an argument. I feared I might lose you before I'd won you back. Hearing you call off the wedding again must have been a knife to his heart."

"Not in the least." She sighed. "He's the one who broke the engagement, Bo." When his jaw dropped, she added, "I was trying my best to tell him that I was breaking up, but it appears that he favors Cee's cooking over mine."

"Cee's cooking? What does Cee's cooking have to do with your engagement?"

She rubbed her bleary eyes. "It's a long story. Cee has been bringing Gideon dinners. I might know the way to win a man's heart is through his stomach, but I've never mastered the skills to do so. I believe Cee used my ineptness to her advantage." She squeezed Bo's arm. "I can't fault her. Her cooking saved me from a very difficult task."

He sat up straighter. "You're serious? *Gideon* broke the engagement?"

"Dead serious, but only because I couldn't get a word in edgewise. That man can talk himself into a frenzy when his conscience hurts him. I went there to break the engagement, but he did all the work."

Bo gathered her even closer and buried his face in her neck. His arms felt like home.

Clearing her throat, she prompted. "Don't you have something to tell me?"

"Me?" He thought for a moment. "I love you?"

"I know that. Something bigger."

"Bigger?" He shook his head. "I'm not good at games, Elly, not after being up all night."

Lowering her voice, she met his gaze. "Why didn't you tell me that Willow wasn't your child?"

He looked straight into her eyes. "You thought she was my daughter?"

"Of course," she said. "It was rather obvious."

"That I fathered Willow?"

"Yes. You knew I had to be tied in knots wondering why a strange woman would drop a three-year-old child at your house and you'd accept her without question."

Shaking his head, he started to chuckle.

"I fail to see the humor in my question."

"Just give me a minute." He tried to wipe the grin off his face. "Willow isn't my child, Elly, and I am sorry that you thought otherwise. Willow's mother was a young woman in my congregation. When I first met her, she was running away from a man who mistreated her. Buck Tarrash. He nearly beat her to death when he learned she was carrying his child.

"She sought refuge with our congregation. She and Willow were taken in by a very kind couple in the church. The couple became like grandparents to Willow, but when Jenna returned to saloon work, the father discovered their whereabouts and threatened to take the child away from her.

"Jenna wanted to run, but she had nowhere to go. Her folks disowned her when she was thirteen. A woman—still a girl, actually—doesn't have too many options at that point.

"Not long after I returned to Berrytop, a gunfight erupted in the bar and Jenna took a bullet. The note asked me to watch over Willow until I could find her a good, God-fearing home, a home where no one knew Jenna's past. She didn't want her choices to reflect on her child.

"So far, I haven't found anyone young enough or inclined to take on an extra mouth to feed. The older couple she earlier lived with had poor health, and though they loved her like a granddaughter, they couldn't take her back."

The world slowly tilted back to normal. "You could have said something."

"I should have, but for some reason it never occurred to me that you'd connect Willow with my ugly past." He gently turned her to face him. "I may have broken promises, lost my way for a while, but you and you alone will be my children's mother. I can't believe you thought it could ever be otherwise."

"Me and the whole town," she grumbled.

"Seriously." He shook his head. "Huh."

Men.

He drew her close to nuzzle her neck. "You smell good." His voice lowered to a whisper. "Bo Garrett is asking—begging—Elly Sullivan to marry him. Can you see past the hurt I've caused to trust me with your heart?"

Smiling, she leaned back in his arms, confident that she could. "Elly Sullivan trusts you implicitly and accepts your proposal."

Elly was only slightly aware of the folks coming and going with covered dishes. The front door banged shut and then reopened every few minutes. Above them, Adele's screams intensified.

Bo held on to Elly tightly, as though she might slip away from him. "I know this isn't the most romantic proposal, but I needed to catch you when you weren't betrothed to Gideon." She felt the breath of his words on her ear.

She swatted him. "What about your church in Parsons? I will follow you wherever you decide to settle, and as far as me being a pastor's wife, I can do that now, and I will, with all my heart."

Drawing back, he met her gaze. "I know you haven't dedicated your life to serve God—"

How could this crucial truth have been missed in their declarations? "I have dedicated my life to serve God, you, and Willow—your whole family. I hadn't realized until recently that He was asking." She marveled that the thought of being a pastor's wife no longer intimidated her. In fact, the thought of serving God in such a gratifying way fit like a comfortable old shoe.

Elly put her hand to Bo's cheek. "You and I have come a long way, and you've made me grow to adore God as a loving, not an angry, Father. Reverend Richardson is good and preaches from his heart. I only pray that he will someday experience the love of God and share that knowledge with his congregation."

"I suppose every person approaches the message in his own way. Richardson is a fine man. He's served the Lord faithfully, but he's nearing his end in the pulpit." Bo shifted and sat up straighter. "Yesterday I stopped by to visit the Reverend. Pa learned much through his teachings, and I wanted to thank him for his service to the community. The Reverend confessed he was slow to regain strength from his last bout with pneumonia. The doctor has, indeed, advised him to reduce his pastoral duties to a trickle. He asked me to take over here."

"Permanently?"

"Odd, isn't it? We were two entirely different people seven years ago. People hated to see us coming because of the mischief that followed. And now we'll be shepherds to this small community."

A bubble of joy rose in her throat. "So you're going to accept the position?"

"I've barely had time to consider the offer. I love my congregation in Parsons, but now that Pa's gone, Ma will need help with the bogs. And I'm thinking you won't want to leave your parents and Adele, plus the little someone she's trying to bring into the world right now. Ma would like to have her grandchildren around, and it's likely Anne won't ever come back. To be honest, now that I'm home, I don't want to leave."

Elly marveled to hear Willow referred to as a grandchild, but that was the Garrett way. No family in all of Berrytop loved better, and the child's spark was endearing to all who knew her. Elly could think of no sweeter calling than to be her mother.

A high-pitched, ear shattering scream interrupted her thoughts. Elly and Bo turned to gape at the second floor window. "Should we be doing something?" he asked.

"Adele's in very good hands with your mother and the doctor at her side. I've been praying as we talked."

"Anyway," Bo continued absently, "now that I have a moment to think, I believe this is what God had in mind all along." He turned and tucked a lock of hair behind Elly's ear. "I want to come home to you and Willow every single night of my life."

Their mouths drew closer. "We should probably tame our kisses while sitting here," she whispered. She would surely melt into her shoes if they didn't.

"Why? I shouted my love to you and to the world not so many years ago."

"We were only kids. Besides, the neighbors will talk, and it's too soon after your father's death, don't you think?"

"Pa loved you." His lips gently touched behind her ear. "And I love you more than words can say."

"Bo..." Her limbs went as weak as a newborn lamb.

The front door burst open and Faye rushed out. "It's a boy!"

Scrambling to her feet, Elly clapped her hands. "A boy!"

Faye wiped her forehead with a cloth. "Doc's getting the scales, but he says he'll weigh in round about six pounds."

Elly's smile faded. "Isn't that small?"

"For a young'un that's this early? Not at all! It's a good weight. He's fine, and he looks just like his pa!"

"Ike must be dancing for joy in heaven!" Elly drew Faye into an exuberant hug. "You must be so proud, Grandma."

Tears brimmed in Faye's eyes, but she smiled like a child at the county fair. Milt hadn't been in the ground but a few hours and already she seemed determined to march on. "Milt said it would be a boy. I imagine he's dancing along with Ike right about now." Turning on her heel, she rushed back into the house, where tiny cries were now coming from the upstairs.

"A boy." Elly sank to the step, wiping tears from her eyes. "A life is taken, and a new life appears." Scooting closer, Elly risked a brief congratulatory kiss. Later, she would more properly show her admiration to the new uncle. "You know what?"

"What?"

"That could have been one of our children being born today, if you'd come home earlier." Here she was nagging already.

A knowing smile brightened Bo's eyes. "Well, I'm home now. I could get Richardson here within the hour to marry us. I say about everyone in town is here or nearby. What do you think?"

"Are you serious?"

"Dead serious. I've waited seven years for this day." Bo stood and pulled her up to join him. "I don't want another thing to interrupt what clearly God desires for us. Besides, the whole town will be dropping by to congratulate Adele soon enough. They can stay for a wedding. Say the word and I'll get Richardson."

There was no doubt in Elly's mind that their union was providentially inevitable. As the baby discovered the power of his lungs, his cries intensified.

"Who needs an hour? I can be ready in thirty minutes." She wasn't about to give him a spare second to change his mind.

Their lips met and her eyes closed in heavenly bliss. The kiss deepened to a silent promise of the forever love they'd sworn to each other so very many years ago. All her prayers had been answered— and who knew what new dreams lay just around the corner?

Everything was about to begin. All in God's good time.

To learn more about Harvest House books and
to read sample chapters, visit our website:

www.harvesthousepublishers.com

HARVEST HOUSE PUBLISHERS
EUGENE, OREGON

Lori Copeland is the author of more than 100 titles. Her beloved novel *Stranded in Paradise* is now a Hallmark Channel Original Movie. Her stories have developed a loyal following among her rapidly growing fans in the inspirational market. She lives in the beautiful Ozarks with her husband, Lance.